New Year's Resolution

by

Samantha Lucas

New Year's Resolution

Cover Art by *R.J.Morris*

The Wild Rose Press
PO Box 706
Adams Basin, NY 14410-0706
Visit us at www.thewildrosepress.com

Publishing History
Scarlet Rose Edition, December 2006
Print ISBN 1-60154-196-1

Published in the United States of America

Dedication

This one's for Pete. Your friendship means the world to me. I would have been lost without you over the last month. Thanks so much for everything.

Chapter One

Caitlyn raised an apple martini to her friends in toast. The two best friends a girl could have, they remained the only two people in the world that knew her secret.

She smiled. "To New Year's resolu—"

"Caitlyn, hon', it ain't even Christmas 'til tomorrow." Valerie smiled and downed another tequila shot.

Caitlyn squirmed in her seat, determined to get this out regardless of how uncomfortable it was. "I realize that, Val. But I have a resolution and I wanted you guys to be the first to know."

She swallowed hard, two sets of eyes glued to her. Which was a funny picture when she thought about it. A giggle bubbled up at the thought of eyes literally glued to her person. Maybe she'd had enough to drink tonight.

Caitlyn shook her head and refocused on her announcement. She'd done little else than think about her secret dilemma since the death of her mother four months ago. Making this decision scared her silly, and the announcement thereof, that she was stalling in a very deliberate fashion. She took a deep breath, and the entire sentence gushed out.

"I intend to divest myself of my stupid cumbersome virginity by midnight New Year's Eve or die trying."

Dead silence greeted her declaration. It was like one of those cartoon moments when you heard crickets. For a time it felt like even the sound system in the club had dimmed so everyone could hear what Caitlyn Monson had to say. A blush crawled all the way from her cheeks to her toes. She downed the rest of her martini and set the glass on the table in front of her and waited.

When frustration and embarrassment got the better of her at last, she guarded herself with arms crossed tight over her chest. "What?"

Valerie ordered another shot. Naomi continued to stare.

"It's not like either of you are virgins. I'm twenty-seven years old. *Twen-Tee-Sev-Ven.*" She emphasized each syllable. "It's very possible that I'm the oldest living virgin on the planet."

"No." Valerie shook her head, her shellacked and polished blonde spikes didn't budge. "No." She raised a finger. "That guy in the movie was forty."

Caitlyn strangled a cry, steeped in aggravation, before it got life. "I'm not in a movie. Let's be serious for a moment. I'm at the point of no return. At twenty-seven, you either go drastic or that's it. Virgin. Spinsterhood. All eternity."

For dramatic effect, she attempted to down the rest of her drink. When she realized she'd already finished it, she sat the glass down again with a pout and licked the single drop she'd gotten from her lips.

"Honey, I'm not saying you should save it for marriage." Naomi pushed flame red hair behind her ear and leaned closer before continuing. "But this seems a little extreme. Don't you think?"

Valerie laughed a little too loudly, and Caitlyn was glad Naomi had agreed to be the designated driver tonight. They needed one. Naomi shot Valerie the look of death. She pouted and shifted in her seat and eyed the bartender for the fiftieth time since they walked in the place.

Caitlyn had to admit, Val's selection tonight was a lot more along her own tastes. The bartender was *fuh-ine* in capital letters. Rich black hair, curled where it brushed his collar, and he had a hard body, great biceps but not overdone. From where she sat in The Cherry Blossom Cantina, his eyes were dark and mysterious, and his smile...lethal.

She knew she had it bad when she had to concern herself with drool. If she got her courage up later, maybe she'd check him out as *the one.* Her mom told her all her life, "When it's the right one, you'll just know it." At twenty-seven and after never having felt the elusive *It,* she wasn't expecting to. But she *was* hoping for a little spark of some sort from the guy she'd let take her virginity.

"I mean, what about love?"

Caitlyn shook her head. She'd forgotten Naomi was still on a tangent and tried to shove her attention back into the conversation.

"What about getting to know someone? Someone like Val might not need the preliminaries, but hon', I think you do."

"Hey! What do you mean, someone like *Val?*" Valerie sat straight in her seat, an earring made out of guitar picks from guys she'd screwed—some famous, most not—dangled from her left ear. "I take offense to that. Maybe you need to go and get fucked. Loosen you up a bit."

She covered Caitlyn's hand with her own.

"Caitlyn's had a rough year; if she wants to end it with a *bang...*" Valerie was obvious in her weak attempt to hold back laughter at her own little joke, "...it's nobody's business but her own. Now, I'm gonna go find that shot girl. I've got a whole day with my family tomorrow and I'm gonna need a real fine hangover to get through it."

Caitlyn watched her meander through the thinning pre-holiday crowd and played with her empty martini glass. "I thought it was the being drunk that got you through the unpleasant and the hangover was the price you paid after."

Naomi shrugged. "I've never understood her logic. Hey, since you brought up tomorrow, come over for dinner?"

4

Caitlyn closed her eyes. *She* hadn't brought up tomorrow but figured that wasn't the point. She wanted to forget that tomorrow was Christmas, but all the decorations, carolers, and yuletides around every corner made it a bit difficult. "No, but thanks."

Naomi groaned. "What are you gonna do? Sit in your apartment all by yourself all day?"

Caitlyn tucked long strands of dark-blonde hair back towards the pony tail it had fallen from. Without ado, it fell right back onto her face. "I plan to go to the cemetery for a while."

She knew what the heavy sigh meant, but Naomi had both her parents and three brothers. There was no way she could begin to understand how alone and lost Caitlyn felt these days. She had no one anymore.

"Look, I'm not interested in Christmas this year." She smiled, raising her eye brows in a festive flirty motion that belied her true feelings. "Just New Year's."

Naomi dropped her head onto her arms folded on the table, a muffled groan rising from the mass of curls. Caitlyn stood up, rubbed her hand in Naomi's wild hair and dropped a kiss on her head before she whispered, "I'll be all right. Now I'm gonna go get another drink. Want one?"

Naomi didn't lift her head but shook it in the negative as it lay on the table. Caitlyn laughed and headed for the bar, scanning the club-slash-restaurant for her platinum, spiky

5

haired friend. Valerie was half-way to wasted and that was never good. Caitlyn had long been Val's caretaker, she imagined their relationship was more than a little co-dependent, but then, she did co-dependent so well.

"Your friend is something else. Is the redhead your driver?"

Caitlyn was a little startled by the personal bent to the conversation the bartender started out of the blue and without prelude, but she figured Val had hit on him and guys Val hit on always thought they had the right to talk with *her* about any and everything. She wondered if he'd taken Val up on whatever she'd offered.

"Uh, yeah." *Eloquent, Caity.* "Can I get a diet coke?"

"Sure."

Figures she'd hit on the one guy in the place I wanted.

Val's usual tastes ran towards musicians, but there was no band here tonight, which left her short on possibilities, and as Caitlyn met gazes with the bartender, she thought Val could have picked a lot worse. She also bemoaned her own loss. No guy would ever choose prudish, uptight Caitlyn over fun loving, easy Val.

She watched him as all her plans died. He moved behind the bar in fluid motion. Muscles pulled and flexed beneath the thin fabric of the navy T-shirt as he grabbed a glass, filled it with ice, soda, and a straw before he delivered it back to her with one of those killer smiles. It was almost like a dance and boy, oh boy, did she wish she could run her fingers over that man's chest.

Maybe I'm drunker than I realized.

Thoughts of men's chests and her fingers were not the norm. She pulled out a five, but the bartender held up a hand to stop her.

"It's on the house. Merry Christmas, sweetheart."

Caitlyn smiled shyly, glad he couldn't read minds but afraid her blush might have given her away, anyway.

"Thanks."

This was where it always broke down for her: she saw a guy, thought he was cute, he seemed nice enough, but then nothing. *Nothing* ever happened from here. She wasn't quite sure what she did wrong. She'd given out her number, gone against her own shy nature to call on the rare occasions she got a number, made herself available.

Sometimes too available, but she wouldn't go back over Don Whitehead again. Some experiences were better left dead.

And here she was, Christmas Eve, virginity in all its glory still in place. Hell, she'd never once gone further than second base and that had been such a fast grope she wasn't sure it counted. "Pathetic."

"You say something, sweetheart?"

Caitlyn shook her head. Her gaze locked in the smoky blue depths of his as he stood behind the bar, drying glasses with a rag and smiling at her like she was the answer to every prayer he ever had, or maybe like she was his dinner. She wasn't sure which, but that look made her heart stutter and caused a breathy laugh to escape her.

Hey, wanna de-virginize me? It was right on the tip of her tongue, but she shook her head. "Nope, I said nothing."

She took her soda, and without haste returned to the safety of her table. How in the world could she lose her virginity if she couldn't even talk to a good looking man?

"Pathetic."

****

Danny Carter leaned against the bar and wondered what the hell he was doing. It was obvious the little blonde hailed from territory far too innocent for the likes of him. Her friend, on the other hand, was far too scary. That girl had anger issues. She was the kind of woman out to hurt a man any way she could. He shuddered at the thought, and his balls recoiled.

Not the sweet one, though. She was the kind a man kept safe. Tucked close to your side, preferably naked, all winter long.

Which means 'not for you.'

He swirled the rag over the glass and added it to the plastic tray behind the bar. Why everything had to breakdown Christmas Eve was beyond him. First, Carl called in sick, leaving him with one option at such short notice. So he filled in as bartender—a skill he hadn't used in long enough that he was sure he'd given more than one person the wrong mix tonight. Thank God everyone was in such good spirits no one had complained yet.

Then the dishwasher spazzed out on him, and as if that weren't bad enough, along came the sweet little blonde in the flirty 'come and fuck me' skirt and shoes with ribbons laced around her ankles like she were a damn present.

He groaned.

A present he'd be more than happy to open. He could almost picture it. First he'd take down her hair and run his fingers through the silky strands. He wondered how far down her back they'd come. Would the fall of hair cover her breasts? *Oh, God.* It was pure torture, but he pictured her naked in the moonlight. Her hair hid full breasts from view as he laid her on the rug by his fireplace. Pressing open her thighs, he viewed her sweet pussy in all its wet, pink glory.

Another groan, and he had to lean against the bar for support. He thought about how he would unbutton and push back the little pink sweater.

Christ. All the girl was missing to complete the Donna Reed look was a strand of pearls.

His mind detoured into the wicked once more. Would her bra match the sweater? Would her nipples?

He cut off the last groan before it could fully come to life. Here he was, Christmas Eve, standing behind the bar of the club he owned—with a raging hard-on for one of his customers. *Businessman of the year, here I come.*

"Hey, baby. Wanna fuck?"

Danny closed his eyes, placed a pleasant smile on his face and turned to face the brash blonde on the other side of the bar. Somewhere along the way, he'd gotten old without even knowing it. That was the only explanation when *wanna fuck* didn't jumpstart your engine anymore. "I think you're drunk. Maybe you should call it a night."

Without a hint of grace, she clambered up onto a bar stool. At one point Danny thought one of her breasts was sure to free itself from the leopard print tank that was about three sizes too small. He shook at the thought and let his gaze slip to the little blonde at the table by the window.

A light snowfall was illuminated by the neon cherry tree in full bloom outside the club and made the perfect backdrop for Little Miss Innocent. She appeared almost angelic. Laughing at something her friend said, her head dropped back and gave Danny a mouthwatering view of her long neck. The desire to suck on it damn near killed him.

"Oh God, not you, too."

Danny twisted his neck at the aggrieved sound until his gaze fastened on the friend.

"Listen, do you want some coffee?"

"Hell, no, I don't want coffee." She placed her knee on the bar stool and leaned over the bar until her face was a mere inch from his. "What do all the guys see in Caitlyn? She's sweet, but she's a mind-numbing bore for someone like you. Goodie-two-shoes doesn't begin to cover it." She walked her fingers over his chest, while Danny did his best not to cringe in a way she'd notice. "She's a virgin, you know." Her smile widened. "I'm not."

Danny's snort of laughter wasn't expected, and he felt bad for it afterward, but she'd taken him off guard with that one. "I bet you're not, honey."

He glanced again from the corner of his eye at Miss Sweet and Innocent, still sitting at the window. What was it about her? She was damned attractive, but then there was the whole ingénue routine. That would usually be enough to send him screaming in the opposite direction, but for some reason—with her it had the opposite effect.

Virgin or not, he didn't know, but he did know she wasn't experience like the women he took to his bed on a regular basis. They knew the score; they didn't expect roses and fairy tale endings from him. Somehow he got the impression that Malibu Skipper would. And more, even if she didn't, the real fear lay in how bad he wanted to give them to her.

As crazy as it sounded, from the moment

she walked into the place, his heart had leapt as if it had waited for her all this time, and the rest of him just hadn't known it had been waiting at all. Well, hell, his body sure knew it now. It was primed and ready to go. He guessed from this point it was a matter of waiting for his brain to climb on board, though he couldn't see how that would ever happen. His brain held his secrets and knew the truth, and his brain would never allow him to hurt pretty Miss Pink Sweater.

"Tell ya what."

Danny held back a sigh and turned his full attention on the woman who now straddled his bar.

"I'll call a cab, if you give me your number."

He caught her finger before she touched his nose with it. "You don't need a cab, Red's driving."

Arms folded over very impressive cleavage that she probably used on a regular basis to get a free ride. She wasn't happy about his rejection. He couldn't blame her, rejection sucked, but he wasn't about to fuck her so she wouldn't feel bad.

"Okay, fine. Better deal for you. How 'bout we screw around in the back for a while and I give you Caitlyn's number."

Now *that* was a tempting offer, but if he wanted Sandra Dee's number, he was pretty damn certain he could get it himself.

"Hey, Val, time to go."

Thank God.

Danny grabbed a clean rag from under the bar and pretended to clean stuff that didn't need to be cleaned while the two women struggled with their loud and obnoxious friend. She argued, the blonde cajoled, but in the end it was Red who laid down the law and the two of them disappeared outside, leaving Little Miss Answer-To-All-His-Dreams alone with him.

Danny smiled at Caitlyn as she gave him a shy smile back. He thought the name suited her, though for some reason, he wanted to call her Caity.

Her blonde hair was pulled away from her face and had so many streaks of color in it, it was wrong to say it was *just* blonde. He didn't think it was something she had done on purpose, though. Somehow Caitlyn seemed natural, from the tip of her blonde head to the tip of those freakin' sexy shoes.

He'd never thought of himself as a man with a foot fetish before, but at the moment, the only clear thought in his head was slowly unwrapping those feet and sucking on her toes.

She was so delicate and sweet, and his arms ached to hold her. As the silence stretched between them, he wondered if she could see the word *stay* written in his eyes.

In an attempt to gain solid ground again, Danny cleared his throat and broke eye contact. It was painful, but it had to be done. "Have a good Christmas. Hope she sobers up by then."

Even though he no longer looked at her

directly, he caught her smile and noticed when she took a step closer.

"Nah, she wants to be drunk. Her family...well, it's kinda complicated."

Danny laughed and met her bright green eyes. *Big mistake.* Those were the kind of eyes a man could spend a lifetime in. He cleared his throat again but still sounded like he had a bad cold when he said, "You're generous. She's out of control."

Caitlyn played with her fingers. Danny noticed she had a nice manicure and shivered at the vision of those fingers circled around his cock. The damn thing hardened further, and he hadn't even gotten to the part where her mouth replaced those fingers.

"Well..." She shrugged.

He knew she wanted more from him. Hell, he wanted to give her more. Wanted to move heaven and earth to make every dream she ever had into a reality. The problem was, he knew who he was in truth and she didn't. He had nothing to offer someone as sweet as she was. Outside of a load of hurt, anyway.

"Well..." Saying Merry Christmas again was pushing it, but stay and come back to my place after I close up...well, wasn't right either. He bit the inside of his cheek to keep any words from slipping out at all.

"Merry Christmas." She gave him a wave, and the sparkle of hope died out of her eyes.

Shit.

"Merry Christmas."

He watched her leave. His cock throbbed, his mind spun, and his heart ached.

Merry Christmas, to be sure.

****

"So?"

Naomi stood by the blue SUV, blowing warm breath into her hands and looking at Caitlyn with a mix of concern and expectancy. Caitlyn shrugged. What had she thought, anyway? A guy like that would never be interested in someone like her. A guy like that took home women like Val. Women who knew the score and knew how to please a man in bed. She had no right to set her sights so high for her first time out and would not make the same mistake twice.

Crap, I wish I'd worn different shoes.

"He didn't want me. Now get in, my toes are numb."

Naomi held open the back door, and Caitlyn slid inside the heated vehicle.

"You'll find someone, Caitlyn, but I so wish you'd rethink this New Year's thing."

She shut Caitlyn's door and climbed in behind the wheel. Caitlyn turned to watch the neon glow of the club grow smaller, and her heart contracted. It was one of those feelings you get when you forget something important, but you just can't remember what. She felt as if she'd left behind a vital piece of herself at The Cherry Blossom, she just didn't know what.

Oh well, she wanted someone to take her virginity, not be prince charming. She'd find him.

Somewhere.

****

A cold wind swept the hem of Caitlyn's long skirt and around her ankles. Even in her boots, her toes felt numb as she trudged through five inches of fresh snow to get to her mother's grave.

The cemetery was busier than she'd expected. She would have thought, on Christmas morning, people would be home with presents to open, family to visit and large breakfasts to eat. Breakfasts of eggs, muffins, fresh squeezed orange juice and whatever other foods you ate on Christmas morning. *Popovers, maybe.* It had been an eternity since she'd had any reason to celebrate at all. What was worse, she couldn't see any reason for that to change in the near future.

The small marker came into view. Overwhelming sadness bore down on her and threatened to crush her under its weight. She blinked back tears, not sure why it mattered, but she didn't want to cry. Not here. Not today. She brushed snow from the top of the tombstone, split her bouquet of roses and placed each half in the special holders on either side of the tombstone that she'd paid three hundred extra for.

"I miss you, mom."

This was the first time she'd been to her mom's grave when she couldn't sit on the ground and talk. She felt awkward as she stood almost looming over the bleak setting. She pulled her coat tighter around her and folded her arms, in the hopes it would keep in her body heat a while longer. The temperature had dipped last night, and this morning's high was as yet to hit thirty five.

"I saw Val and Naomi last night. Naomi asked me to her place for Christmas dinner, but I think I'll stay home." Her breath puffed in a white cloud as she spoke. She pulled her scarf up higher. "I didn't buy a tree or put up any decorations this year. Didn't see the point. Mom, I don't know what to do without you. I'm not even sure who I am anymore."

She did a little shuffle in an attempt to keep the cold at bay longer and wondered if Naomi had a point when she called her clinically depressed. But her whole world had changed and she felt lost. Adrift. Like she had no anchor in life anymore, no direction. Her job held no satisfaction, but then it never had. Desk clerk at the local no-tell motel was what she did to keep the roof over her head—and her mom's. She guessed maybe now she could pick an actual career. Something she'd do because she had passion for it.

But then, she didn't feel passion for anything right now.

"Caitlyn. Is that you?"

17

The soft voice sent tingles over her near frozen skin. She had the collar on her coat wrapped around her ears and a scarf wrapped around the lower part of her face. Include the hat she had on and all that was visible were her eyes. How the hell anyone would recognize her was beyond her, but as she turned she already knew who would be there. She couldn't imagine how or why, though. The only way the bartender from the Cherry Blossom would be standing behind her was if she'd slipped 'round the bend and was hallucinating big time.

She squinted against the cold wind, which blew in her face now that she shifted directions. Sure enough—tall, dark and not interested stood before her.

"Hi." Her voice was muffled behind the layers of her scarf, but she smiled and hoped he could tell by her eyes alone that she was glad to see him.

"Merry Christmas."

Again with the Merry Christmas? Could the man say anything else? After today would he go with happy New Year, then happy Valentines? Did small holidays like Groundhog Day and Presidents' day make it into his routine?

She mumbled a Merry Christmas back, and then the two of them stood there much like fourth graders at their first dance. She caught his glance over her shoulder at the tombstone and the fleeting emotion that passed in his smoky eyes. Somehow the small action comforted her. *How bizarre is that?*

"Family?"

Tears brushed her lids, and she blinked them away. She didn't want to cry in the first place, but the last thing she wanted to do was cry in front of him. "My mom."

"I'm sorry."

How many times had she heard those words. Enough so that they seemed empty, but not from him. From him they almost felt like an embrace. She shook her head to chase away all the feelings—bad or good, it was too much—and wiped at a tear before it froze to her cheek.

"Cancer. She'd been sick a long time, so I think, for her, it was good."

His smile softened, and he gestured with his head in a direction north of where they stood. "Ex-wife."

"I'm sorry," came out with a gasp before she could stop herself.

He shrugged and held out his hand. "Danny, by the way. I don't think we got to names last night."

A smile came upon her. It wasn't the usual type, either. It was the kind of smile a person felt down deep. Odd, but good. Almost like a spring thaw. She placed her gloved hand in his, and it was as if she'd been born to fit her hand with his that way. It was one of those things no one else would understand and probably didn't make any logical sense. To Caitlyn, however, it was as if the final piece of a puzzle slipped into place or the planets aligned or something else as crazy. It was the moment she'd waited a lifetime for. Just like that. No fanfare. No sky writing. It just...happened.

"Caitlyn Monson. Nice to meet you, Danny."

He held her hand longer than necessary, and when he released it, he smiled as if he had decided something important all of a sudden. She swore she saw a weight slide off him. Had he felt what she had?

"You want to go get some coffee, Caitlyn Monson?"

She smiled in return, not that he knew, since her mouth was still covered by the scarf, but that had its purposes. There was no way he could tell how much she blushed as she replied with a soft, "I'd love to." She knew right then that the rest of her life had begun.

Chapter Two

The twenty-four hour diner on Magnolia was the only restaurant open in the small town on Christmas morning and was therefore packed. Caitlyn realized she'd stepped right into a scene from the *Santa Clause* as the tables were filled almost to exclusion with men and kids. The entire drive over from the cemetery, Caitlyn second guessed herself. It was just coffee, but it so wasn't *just* coffee. She wanted Danny to be the one. Her first.

He was kind and handsome, had a great body that she couldn't wait to see naked and his eyes crinkled around the edges when he smiled.

She liked Danny.

Filled with nervous energy, she shifted from foot to foot while they waited for a table. She watched Danny from beneath her lashes and hoped he couldn't figure out what she was doing. She liked the way his dark hair hung, was a little shaggy, thick and wavy, liked the way he wore a turquoise band around his left thumb and liked the way he smelled of musk and cinnamon. Yeah, Danny would be perfect.

Sure, she didn't know his life plans, his

21

credit rating or his bank balance, but she didn't think the occasion called for that kind of knowledge. More important, she felt like her heart knew him—had always known him—and nothing was more important to her than that.

"You okay?"

Well, at least it wasn't Merry Christmas.

She wondered how he'd react if she said, *Fine. Was wondering however, if you'd take my virginity*—eyelash bat—*please.*

She coughed to dislodge thoughts of hot, sweaty sex from her brain and the lust-inspired lump from her throat. "Fine."

He smiled.

She smiled.

Both looked away.

Caitlyn twirled a loose strand of hair around her finger. She couldn't remember the last time she'd done that, but it was somewhere around her eighth birthday. However, the need to keep her hands busy was an imperative, and that seemed a better alternative than to run her hand over his suede jacket to see if those bulges were all bicep or not.

"We have a booth in the back ready for you."

Caitlyn snapped to attention as the hostess led them through the dining room. Danny put his hand at the small of her back as they wound between tables and waitresses until they reach a horseshoe-shaped booth in the back corner big enough to seat six.

"Are you sure you don't need this for a

bigger group?" Caitlyn was appalled at how high pitched her voice sounded, but she wasn't sure she could handle Danny in a booth with the only thing between them dead space. She had sort of hoped for one of those tables for two in the middle of the dining room. The kind you'd hate to get on any other occasion but that was perfect for this one.

"You guys were next on the list. Don't worry about it." Caitlyn's eyes widened as the woman gave Danny a quick once-over. "Enjoy your meal."

Pulling off his jacket, he tossed it up on the raised ledge behind the booth then turned to help Caitlyn with hers. She was still sort of numb, not from the cold but from the thought of sitting in a booth with Danny.

You want to have sex with him, but you don't want to sit in a booth with him?

She smiled, let him take her coat and yanked the skirt of the long black cotton dress she'd worn out of the way while she scooched into the booth. She tucked hair behind her ear and pretended fascination with the menu but didn't miss that Danny hadn't gotten in on the other side, yet. Instead, he still stood beside her. Keeping a lock on the nervous laughter, she gazed up at him.

A wicked smiled crept across his face as if he knew everything she'd thought all along. "It's kind of a big booth. Thought I might get lost all the way over there."

She couldn't hold back the little bubble of breathy laughter this time, and it mortified her. "Oh."

Since she had never been fast on her feet with a comeback, she slid over in mute submission to allow him the space beside her. She'd left him more than enough room, but he slid all the way into the booth until his thigh met hers.

His hard, muscular thigh.

Caitlyn wondered how it would feel to run her hands over his entire body. If all of his body was so hard and muscular. Before she could stop herself, she pictured him naked, on her bed, her hands caressing that thigh, her mouth... "Oh God!"

"Something wrong, sweetheart?"

"Merry Christmas! Can I get you guys some coffee to start?"

Oh, thank the Lord. "I'll have coffee." *And anything else to keep my hands, mouth, and thoughts busy.*

"Coffee sounds good, thank you."

After their waitress left, Danny placed his arm across the back of the booth in a casual move that seemed more normal than practiced, but that she'd seen done in old TV shows all the time. It had the effect of making her feel small and safe and feminine, as well as surrounded by his heat and his scent. Internally, she groaned.

"Are you hungry, Caitlyn?"

Hungry? God yes. She gave herself a mental

slap. *He meant food, you nutcase.* "Uh, I'm not sure."

If anything, she swore the man moved closer. Then, with his free hand, he picked up one of hers. Frissons of fear, lust and need skated her spine. She shivered without warning. He entwined their fingers, closing his hand around hers in another move that seemed so natural it made her heart ache and thighs tremble, all at the same time.

"I'm hungry." He looked into her eyes, his normal grey-blue had grown dark. "Starved, actually."

She had the crazy notion he wasn't talking about food, and there came that stupid giggle again. She swallowed hard, forced her gaze from his and put it back on the menu.

"They have good French toast." Her voice was high pitched and squeaky again, and she wanted to cry. She'd never be able to do this. She wasn't man eater material. She was Olivia Newton-John in Grease *before* the big switch at the end. Only her big switch wasn't happening. She was doomed to life as a virgin, and that was that. Might as well get used to it.

Danny once again questioned his sanity. He'd gone to Margo's grave this morning, as he did on every holiday and her birthday, with the sole purpose of receiving the very effective reminder of what a loser he was—to remind himself that the one woman he ever tried to love had thought death a better alternative.

It shocked the living hell out of him when, in the midst of his morbid obsessive thoughts, the hairs on the back of his neck prickled and his cock twitched in response to her presence. And that was before he'd even seen her. How the hell was *that* possible?

He'd known though, within a heartbeat, his body's reaction could only mean one thing. He started a search for her. When his eyes rested on a petite black bundle from head to foot, he knew he'd found her. Knew he wasn't alone, and even for a time, knew there was hope in a world usually so austere.

The waitress set coffee in front of each of them, apologized for being swamped and said she'd be right back. He let go of Caity's hand with great reluctance but figured she'd need it to open sugar packets or pour milk or whatever it was she did with her coffee. He opened and poured one packet of artificial sweetener into his and took a long sip.

"So how long ago did your mother pass?"

He cringed. *Oh, way to go, Romeo.* He wanted to kick himself when he saw the sadness flash in her eyes. Lord have mercy, but he wanted to protect her from that sadness. He ran a hand though his hair and redirected his focus to the dark liquid in his mug. "Never mind. None of my business."

To his shock, she placed a gentle hand atop his. Her touch made his heart skip beats, made his breath trip and, bottom line, made him hard.

"It's okay. I'm not used to people asking, is all. It's been four months, but like I said, she was sick for several years before that." She took a sip of her coffee. "Wasn't much of a life, anyway."

The catch in her voice broke his heart. He'd never been close to anyone in his life—not even Margo, to tell the truth—so he didn't know what it felt like to lose someone he loved. He did, however, feel consumed by a need to somehow make it right for Caitlyn, even as he knew it wasn't possible. "You must have loved her very much."

She smiled, though it seemed sad. "She was all I had. All either of us had, to be honest. My dad wasn't ever in the picture, and mom never dated again, so it was the two of us."

He'd never know why he did it, but he took her dainty hand and kissed the tips of each finger. It had probably started out as a gesture of comfort, but before his lips even touched the first tip it turned into something more. Her green eyes went molten as he sucked her ring finger just barely between his lips.

"So have you guys had a chance to decide?"

Oh, hell yeah. I'll have the blonde, with a side of whip cream, thank you very much.

Caitlyn swallowed hard and tore her gaze from Danny's. With a forced smile that she hoped looked somewhat realistic, she ordered French toast and orange juice. Danny ordered an omelet with every type of meat imaginable.

27

She guessed he had a big appetite. She wasn't sure she'd even be able to eat what she ordered, with him sitting so close and constantly finding reasons to touch her.

What she'd read in the books she ordered on-line had not prepared her for the reality. She'd read about being hot and achy and *wet,* but didn't think she'd ever experience it in such fine detail. She'd read about desire and chemistry, but God above, if he didn't make love to her, she might die from the want of it.

Now the problem was, how on earth did one go from breakfast conversation to "Take me home and fuck me. Please." Her mother had always been one for manners, and they were engrained in permanent ink at this point.

She drank her coffee and watched the man with as much subtlety as she could. She was utterly fascinated by him. By every ripple, every hair, every inch of skin. His Adam's apple moved as he swallowed coffee, his fingers played with the empty sweetener packet, his eyes burned whenever they roamed over her.

Somewhere between the nervous breakdown over the booth and the conversation over their meal, which she was thankful had turned more relaxed, Caitlyn decided she *could* do this. That she *would* do this. It was what she wanted, and she was under the impression that a guy wanted sex all the time, so Danny would be okay with it, right?

She swallowed while he pulled a few bills

from his wallet. "Oh!"

Snapped back to the present, she grabbed her purse, but his hand clamped down over hers. His breath tickled her ear as he leaned close. "Let me."

She turned her head to find Danny's mouth so close, it wouldn't have taken more than a twitch before their lips would be together. She stared into his eyes, caught in the grey-blue storm inside them. Wanting, wondering and wishing for so many things they seemed impossible.

"Danny." She whispered his name, but wasn't certain why. She swore he was about to kiss her. She wetted her bottom lip eagerly and saw him swallow hard. His hand brushed strands of hair away from her face. "Danny, please."

He pressed his lips to her temple and whispered a harsh, "Darlin' I'm in too deep here." Then he pulled away, took the check and the money and went to the cashier. He didn't look back so he never saw the stunned look on Caitlyn's face or the single tear that slipped her guard as she watched him leave her.

****

Outside it had started to snow again. Caitlyn fiddled with her keys, any excuse to keep this from coming to an end yet. She didn't know what she wanted for the rest of her life, but she knew with certainty she did not want to be alone. For the rest of the day or the rest of her life.

"Danny, I..." she looked away. He'd already rejected her once. Twice if she counted the night before at the bar. Glutton for punishment she wasn't. "Never mind. Thanks for breakfast."

He opened his mouth, but she put a gloved hand over it.

"If you're about to say Merry Christmas, save it. I won't be having one so save your well wishes for someone who cares. Do you want to know what I'll be doing the rest of the day?"

Emotions had run high all day, and Caitlyn knew when she was at a loss to them. This was one of those times. She didn't stop long enough for him to answer before venting months worth of pent up anger and frustration on him.

"Nothing. Absolutely freaking nothing! I'll go home where I haven't decorated or even bought a tree. I won't have a Christmas dinner with turkey and mashed potatoes, which by the way I love, and I won't have a single present to open and there won't be hot chocolate and *Miracle On 34th Street* later in the night, and there won't be any Christmas cookies for dessert."

The steam that fueled her outburst turned cold, and she finished on a sob. "Which by the way I also love."

Danny took her into his arms and held her while the tears she'd forced back all day won their valiant battle for freedom. His tenderness only served to bring on more tears, and before she could help herself she clung to him and sobbed four months worth of tears. Three years if she were truthful.

"I'm s-so s-sorry." She sniffled as she tried to pull out of his arms, but he wouldn't let her. His body heat warmed her against the slight wind that picked up. It blew snow on them as they stood in the parking lot clinging to one another like horny teenagers facing a curfew.

"Don't be. I'd guess you've held those a long time."

She nodded and tried to wipe her nose with some dignity. She wished now she'd listen to all those times her mom told her to carry tissue. Apparently, Danny had listened to his mom, because after he unlocked the big black pick up, he pulled some from the glove box and handed them to her. She took them and averted her gaze. "I must look horrible."

He pulled off one of his leather gloves and brushed the side of her face.

"No. You're beautiful. Plain and simple."

Caitlyn used another tissue to grab leftover tears from her eyes, then met Danny's gaze. She didn't want this to be over. She didn't want to go home to nothing. *With* nothing. She wanted to go home with Danny. In a burst of courage she reached out and touched his face.

It wasn't as satisfying as she'd hoped since she'd forgotten to remove her glove.

With a groan, she pulled it off and threw it to the ground. She cupped his cheek and

searched his eyes, not at all sure what she was
about to do but rushing in headlong anyway
before she could chicken out and ruin the best
shot she had at happy. "Danny, please don't toss
me aside. Not today. Aren't you lonely, even a
little?"

He closed his eyes as if she'd caused him
great pain, and she was sorry about that, but
the loss of connection brought *her* great pain.
She almost released him, almost stepped away,
almost gave up, but when his eyes opened, they
were full of heat and fire and passion and she
felt it to her bones.

"I can't promise you a picket fence and a
puppy or even a turkey dinner and mashed
potatoes." He entwined their fingers again. "But
do you want to come home with me, Caity?" He
laughed beneath his breath. The sound was as
quiet as the hushed reverence that hung in the
air around them. "I might be able to round up
some cocoa and some Christmas cookies." He
swallowed. "Please, say yes."

Caitlyn's heart cried even as she trembled
with a mixture of cold and excitement. She had
no idea where this ride would take her, but she
could think of no reason on this earth why she
should miss it.

****

Caitlyn was impressed by how warm and
inviting Danny's home was. It was a small brick
Tudor style in a nice neighborhood on a tree
lined street. She wondered what he had against

picket fences and puppies because in her mind, he looked all set up for them.

He took her coat and hung it on a hook alongside his in the entry hall, Caitlyn asked sheepishly if she could leave her boots there, too, as her toes were once again frozen. Danny smiled and pulled off his own boots then threw them into a box that appeared to be there for that purpose. Caitlyn's followed his, and she wriggled her numb toes inside two pair of socks.

Grabbing her by the hand, he led her away from what looked like a formal living room. It also looked like nobody ever went in there. They went through the dining room to the right and then the kitchen, ending in an open expanse of high ceiling, full length window, extremely comfortable great room.

"I added this when we bought the place. Never was too much for the stuffy formality Margo was so crazy for. This was my space."

He rubbed the back of his neck and opened the fridge. Caitlyn did *not* look at his ass when he bent over. Well, at least not for long.

"Want a beer?" He peered over his shoulder and gave her a wink. "Or I could make you an apple martini if you like."

She laughed, feeling more comfortable now that she was here. The retained heat from his house seeped into her bones, made her feel warm and her skin tingle. Although she supposed that could be pure Danny.

"Beer's fine, but soda's better. If you've got

it."

"Coming right up."

She walked past a peninsula counter that separated the kitchen from the family room. Even through her socks, she felt the temperature change when she went from the cool marble tiles of the kitchen to the plush sage green carpet of the great room. Two seconds in the room and she was impressed with how homey it was. It wasn't the kind of place you'd expect a bachelor to live in, but it was obvious no woman lived here either. She liked his choice of artwork, mostly large poster-type art of the ocean and woods. Several were at sunset, and all were matted and framed.

On one wall, was a canoe. She raised a brow at that and moved on. He had several bookcases, filled with a variety of books. She saw poetry, non-fiction self-help type books and tons of fiction, an assortment that ranged from thrillers to sci-fi.

"There's a switch by the fireplace. Want to turn it on?"

He was pouring her soda into a glass when she looked back at him and nodded. It only took her a moment to find the switch, and the large stone fireplace that consumed a whole wall roared to life. She moved her hand over the ragged edges of the stones, admiring the variation of textures and colors when Danny snuck up behind her.

"I hand-picked all of those. Went up to the

quarry and drove the shit out of those guys, going over almost every stone just to find the right ones."

He placed his hand beside hers against the stone. She became breathless at the so-near-so-far action always going on between them.

"You did a great job. It's incredible."

"Thanks."

Danny couldn't take another minute of this torture. He wanted to kiss her but feared he'd never be able to stop at one kiss. Memories of Margo invaded his thoughts, and he shoved them back hard.

She was never happy here. He guessed she'd never been happy anywhere, and though he wished he could say it hadn't been his fault, he blamed himself almost as much as she did. If only he'd been better. *More.* If only he'd been able to understand her and reach into the darkness she kept around herself day and night.

He handed Caitlyn the glass of soda. Against common sense, he brushed her fingers as she reached for it. He could fast become addicted to the way she made him feel. Even from the brief contact his cock hardened and his heart sped up.

She followed him to one of his old grey chenille sofas that flanked the fireplace. He loved these sofas. He'd bought them with the notion of cuddling on a cold winter's night. It hadn't ever worked out that way. Margo wasn't a cuddler, and the women he did bring home, well, *cuddling* wasn't on the agenda.

Lowering himself into one corner, he reached up for her drink and set it on the table beside him then reached back for her and tugged her into his lap onto his flaming erection. He breathed slow and deep and tried to think of anything that would keep his mind off Caity naked. She was killing him. No. She wasn't doing it at all. He was doing it to himself.

She was the hottest woman he'd met in forever. That damn sweet and innocent streak only making her more desirable if that was at all possible, but he didn't want to hurt her. More to the point, he didn't want to be hurt again. He didn't want to trust a woman again, who would soon realize he wasn't good enough. Maybe if he told Caity from the get go, then the inevitable blow up wouldn't be so bad. But with her in his lap, the sweet curve of her ass pressed firm against his hard-on, and the soft scent of her surrounding him, her mouth so close...

He let his fingers wander over the exposed skin of her neck and shoulders. Thankfully, the scoop neckline of her dress, though modest enough, was very accommodating to such explorations.

"Ah, Caity. You'll be the death of me." He whispered the words like an oath against her neck. She smelled so good. So soft. Like tea roses and gardenias and vanilla. He wanted to devour her, wanted to sink his fingers deep inside her heat and feel her pussy weep over him. He wanted to know if he made her half as wet as she made him hard.

Tipping her back into his arms, he was ready to claim her mouth and then her body. He couldn't wait another minute. He had to know her taste, how her nipples would feel in his mouth. Needed to have her surrounding his cock, squeezing him, making him come.

Caitlyn laughed, a little hysterical sound that bubbled up as another bout of nervous energy consumed her. She wiggled against those thighs she'd been so enamored of earlier. Danny's touch was soft and sexy as he brushed the swells of her breasts over the top of her dress. He made her so hot, she thought she would explode. His eyes darkened and churned like the sea as the storm took it. His lips were so close. He was going to kiss her, she knew it. Then he'd make love to her, and she'd finally know what it meant to be a woman. To have a man's body connected with hers in such an intimate fashion. She couldn't wait.

But her nerves took over, and before she knew what she was even thinking, she horrified herself as she blurted out, "I'm a virgin!"

She closed her eyes, and shame washed over her. Not because she was a virgin, after all, everyone started out as one, but more by her lack of finesse and ability to handle sexual situations with men. She should have prepared herself better. The few books she'd read had made her squirm uncomfortably, and she'd given up on that notion. She figured whoever took her virginity would teach her all she needed to know, but she should have checked out books from the library, gone to on-line chats, taken a class at the community college. In this day and age, there was no excuse for someone to be as naive as she was, and that was what ultimately embarrassed her to death.

The light brush of his fingertips crossed her cheek, and as she looked back into his eyes, they were so full of tenderness that she wanted to cry. "Are you going to throw me out now?"

His laugh sent his heated breath over her skin. He smelled of coffee and mint, and her stomach did a little flip as she clutched the front of his shirt, hoping to stay a while longer.

"Not at the moment, sweetheart. But why don't we start with why you're here and what you expect from me."

He didn't push her from his lap. In fact, he sort of cuddled her closer. Did she have the courage to go through with this? She bit her lower lip, her heart beat so hard behind her ribcage she thought for certain it would end up bruised.

"I don't want to be a virgin anymore. I want to know what it's like to love a man—physically, mind you—not emotionally, so don't go thinking I'm trying to trap you or anything."

She threw that in fast before he had a chance to freak out on her and think she had him set up in her mind as Mr. Right. She wasn't convinced such a man existed, and even if he did, her little virginity problem was taking up all her emotional bandwidth at the moment. Mr. Right's existence, or lack thereof, was a problem for another day.

"I just want de-virginized." She closed her eyes again and added, "Preferably by someone nice."

She didn't take offense when she heard him snicker, since he pulled her closer in his arms at the same time. He pressed a kiss to the top of her head, then that rich voice of his washed over her. "Can I ask why you've waited 'til now just to throw it at the first guy you see?"

She pulled back, wiggled a bit to get balance, and with indignation pooling in her belly, she addressed his little misconception. "You are *not* the first guy I've seen. Though you are the first one I've been attracted to in a very long time."

There went all her indignation, because in a way, he was right. He was the first guy she'd seen since making her decision and declaring her resolution, but he didn't need to know that.

"I feel comfortable with you. My heart trusts you. And the reason I've waited so long was just one of those 'life passing you by while you were busy with other stuff' things. First it was college—which didn't take, by the way—and when I did date, I wasn't very good at it. It was uncomfortable, and I never had anything to say. I felt like a joke and rarely got asked on a second date. My mom always said when it was right, I'd know. Well, it never felt right. Then she got sick, and my whole life turned into taking care of her. Now, maybe I want a reminder that I didn't die with her. I want to feel alive for a change. Is that so wrong?"

He tugged her close to his chest again. It didn't feel like a sexual move. It felt protective, and she felt comforted—taken care of. It had been far too long since she'd felt like that.

"I'm not a nice guy, Caity. I don't want to add breaking your heart to my list of sins."

She looked up into his stormy eyes. *She* thought he was a nice guy, and in her book, nothing else mattered. "I'm not asking for marriage or even a commitment past the sex. Just show me what it's like. You are attracted to me, aren't you? A little anyway?"

His laughter rumbled through his chest and reverberated through her body. She put her hands against his shoulders to prop herself up away from him. "What's so funny?"

"First lesson, sweetheart." He took her hand and placed it beneath her, flat on the enormous bulge in his jeans. She gasped. His eyes darkened. "That's not a *little* bit of attraction, honey. I want you so bad I'm expecting permanent damage from the blood loss to my brain."

A small smile played at her lips. His passionate declaration restored some of her courage, and the reality of her hand on his penis...she swallowed...well, she found herself wanting to explore. "Can I see it?"

He blinked, slapped a hand to his forehead and dropped his head back against the sofa. A moment later, he grabbed her wrist and pulled her hand out from where she was so enjoying it. She frowned almost to the point of a pout.

"Woman, you're here to kill me, aren't you?"

"No. I, well, I've never, well, I mean I guess I could have—"

Danny's hand pressed against her mouth with gentle force. "No. You can't *see* it. If I take it out right now, your virginity will be history in three point two seconds."

She giggled.

He scowled.

"Okay, listen, sweetheart. We need a plan here. Believe me, parts of me are more than willing to help out with your little problem, but my brain is screaming 'back up' really, really loud."

He pressed his lips against her forehead for a long time. "You're sure about this?"

It was one of those moments when you know your entire life is about to change. Caitlyn sobered, then touched his cheek even as she ached to kiss him.

"Never been more sure about anything."

He took a deep breath, held it for a second, then released it slow and even. "Then I'm in, Caity, but we're gonna go slow."

Chapter Three

Caitlyn snuzzled down in Danny's lap, filled with pure contentment from head to foot. "Slow's good. I had kinda hoped it would last like maybe a half hour or so, but Val says most guys don't make it past five minutes."

His body tensed, and a strange sound strangled in his throat. Caitlyn reached out to touch his larynx, but he caught her hand too fast. She found everything about the man fascinating, and she wanted to touch him everywhere, not just the private places.

"Okay, first, some rules."

Her brow furrowed at his commander-in-chief tone. She didn't like the sound of that, but having her first time with Danny felt right. It was the elusive feeling she'd spent her entire adult life in search of, and she wasn't about to turn her back on this opportunity.

"One, I am *not*, repeat N-O-T taking your virginity today. It's Christmas, for Christ's sake—a day for virgins—and you will remain one for the duration."

"But..."

"No buts." He held up a finger and touched

the tip of her nose. "I want to give us both a chance to make sure this is what you want."

"It is."

God, she couldn't remember another time she felt more whiny. Not since she was five anyway, but she was on fire and in his lap—so close and so intimately connected to his wonderful bulge. It all conspired against her strength of will. Plus, she wondered if she'd mentioned yet that she was *twenty-seven* and not getting any younger.

"I know you think it is, but what if this is some post-traumatic mourning phase?"

Ooh, he made her mad with that one. This man was not about to tell her what she could or could not do with her body, nor did he have any right to assume he knew her mind better than she did. She tried to squirm off his lap, but he was quicker and pulled her back down, holding her tight.

"I don't want you to hate me, Caity." He pressed his forehead to hers. "I couldn't take that."

All the anger drained from her so fast, it was hard to remember that she'd been mad in the first place. She cupped his face in her palms. "I like when you call me Caity. Only my mom ever did. It makes me feel special"

She sighed. Under the circumstances, she should just accept the fact that she'd go along with whatever he wanted, because he was *the one* and there was no way around it.

"How slow?" She tucked hair behind her ears and licked her lips. "'Cause I kinda had this whole New Year's resolution thing going."

Danny chuckled—a rich, warm sound—and she loved the way it traveled through her body as if he was a part of her. "I think I can have you de-virginized by New Year's, if that's what you want. But right now, I really need to kiss you."

She ran her tongue over her bottom lip expectantly. "Okay. Please."

He framed her mouth with his thumbs, brushing the lower lip with one of the pads. "Something tells me this will be the greatest kiss of my life." His voice was soft and reverent, and Caitlyn hadn't a doubt in the world he meant it. He brought his lips closer. "You terrify me." Then his mouth covered hers, and she lost any ability to think.

At first his lips were soft, gentle, the brush of butterfly wings. He pressed them against hers as if he wanted to taste her, and her heart fluttered. Her hands stilled on his cheeks, and he mirrored her position. His thumbs grazed the surface of her face.

"You taste like heaven, Caity."

His lips brushed hers again, but this time he nipped her top lip, then sucked on the lower. Caitlyn captured his lip between hers and ran her tongue over it. She loved it when he moaned against her mouth. His fingers slid across her neck, and both hands moved until he cradled her head, tilted it, and kissed her mouth like he needed her more than food, water, or air.

Caitlyn felt achy, hot and so very wet. She squeezed her thighs together against the need and wondered if Danny was anywhere near done taking it slow. She wanted to touch him, wanted to see him naked. She surprised herself with the fact that she wanted to take his penis in her mouth and taste him. She wanted to see it soft, wanted to watch it grow, harden, and lengthen. She wanted to touch and taste him everywhere. A groan escaped her when she realized her own thoughts were making her more horny.

She wrapped her arms up around his neck, her fingers playing in the hair that curled at his collar, which she found very sexy. She found everything very sexy if it included her and Danny. She wondered how much longer before his hands moved below her chin. Her breasts felt heavy and her nipples painfully erect, and she swore to every deity she could think of that if he didn't get her naked soon, she would be a victim of spontaneous combustion.

Too much.

With a groan, she pulled her mouth from his. "Danny, slow isn't working for me. I want to touch you."

Danny didn't respond with words because he knew she was too aroused to listen. Slow wasn't working for him, either; he was about ready to explode. He never would have guessed in a million years that a chaste kiss could be so damned erotic. Slow was the single option in his mind, but he understood what his little Caity needed and he could certainly relate. He tipped her body down into the sofa, leaned atop her and pressed their bodies together. With her body captured beneath his, he felt a primal heat surge within.

My woman. Mine.

He didn't know Caity well enough to know if she were the type of woman who knew her own mind, or if she was one of those fly-by-the-seat-of-her-pants types, changing her mind faster than the traffic lights went from green to red. He was all in favor of being the one to initiate her to sex, but he wasn't about to take advantage of her and sit back and blame her for it if it all blew up in their faces.

"I need you too, Caity, but be patient with me."

His hand smoothed the side of her dress to her hip, and he pulled her hot pussy closer to his cock. It jumped, as if it somehow recognized its mate. He groaned, wrapped his hand around to the flat of her back and pulled her whole body completely underneath him.

His mouth went back to work on hers. She arched against him in need. Her breasts pressed against his chest, nipples hard and evident beneath the thin cotton of her dress. He wanted to taste them, wanted to suck them and see if he could make her come by that action alone.

She moaned and arched against him again, he tipped her head back further, and with a tentative touch, licked the seam of her lips. She opened for him, and he swept in, claiming her mouth for himself alone. Her tongue was enthusiastic to welcome him, and her sweet, low groan made him ever harder.

Slow. Take it slow. S-L-O-W. Slow.

The words became a mantra in his head as his tongue mated with hers and he imagined what it would feel like to fill her in other places as well. His chest swelled with pride, knowing he would be her first. No other man had ever aroused her, ever touched her the way he planned to touch her.

Her leg wrapped around his, her pussy thrust against his cock, and Danny cursed and blessed in the same breath the layers of clothes between them. Both arms wrapped tight around her. *Mine,* his heart chanted. His brain told him to go take a cold shower, and his cock said, *now goddamnit!*

He knew she was wet, he could feel her heat, wanted to melt into it. "I'm gonna take it slow, Caity. *Slow.*"

She looked up at him with big green eyes, darkened by desire and maybe a little confused by the power of her own need. She nodded and brought her hungry mouth back to his. This time there were no preliminaries. She slid her tongue into his mouth, found his and sucked it back into her mouth.

God almighty. He would never make it.

Caitlyn loved the way Danny's weight pressed her into the sofa. It thrilled her, enticed her, and made her feel gloriously feminine. She sucked on his tongue, listened to him groan and arched her body closer. She was like a half-starved animal; she *needed* his touch, his kiss, more than she wanted it. It was as if she'd die without it.

Boy, when mom was right, she was right.

Up until she'd met Danny, she'd never been sure about anything. Now, she knew what it was like to just *know.*

Maybe it was because her mom had been so sick for so long and Caitlyn had no one else in her life to give or receive affection from that she felt so starved for it. She and Naomi exchanged hugs on occasion, but they were always stiff, almost business-like, and Val... there was no way in hell Val would let anyone touch her.

Well, not unless they had a dick, anyway.

No matter how it happened, she felt starved. Now with Danny's arms around her back, his tongue in her mouth, and his *really* hard, *quite* large package pressed against her labia, she felt like the sharks at the zoo at lunch time. She needed to ravage him until there was nothing left.

His thigh slipped between hers, a move that caused the bulge in his jeans to fit more securely between her legs. She moaned and hated him in that moment for his damned "take it slow" motto. How many other women had he been with? She bet he never took it *slow* with any of them.

Breathless, she broke away from his kiss.

"Please, Danny. Just do it. I feel desperate—*frantic*—and it scares me."

His hand cradled her neck, his dick pressed harder into her. *Is it at all possible it's still getting bigger?* She didn't have time to find an answer for that, Danny captured her mouth without a word to tell her he'd stop going slow. Tongues swirled over one another until he trapped hers. He sucked on it with a soft, gentle, wave-like motion that would have brought her to her knees if she were on her feet. She was overheated and didn't think the fireplace was to blame.

When he stopped kissing her, he pulled back enough so that air rushed between them, she felt bereft, exhausted, overwhelmed and a myriad of other things she couldn't name at the moment. She let her head fall back against the sofa, her soft pants and occasional moans mixed with his in the otherwise silent room.

"I need to get up." His words were stiff, pained, and she wanted to cry.

"Now?"

When he actually did push away from her, she closed her eyes to the pain of it.

"Sweetheart, we need a new plan, 'cause I think your right. Slow will *not* work."

****

Caitlyn felt nosy. While Danny drove into the next town to find a grocer still open, she snooped around his house. It was a nice house, though she could tell he spent all his time in the great room. The living room, dining room and den all looked like showrooms not homes. They were clean—she assumed he had maid service—and nicely decorated. Albeit a bit formally for her taste.

Who knew a bartender did so well?

It was odd to think of Danny married, sharing this house with a woman he'd made such a huge commitment with. She wondered at the stark formality of the house. Was it possible they loved and laughed here? It didn't feel that way to her, and the other thing that struck her as odd was that there was a lot of beautiful artwork in his home, but no personal photos. Not of a mom, dad, brother or sister. None of girlfriends, or his ex-wife. Not even of a dog. Maybe he kept them all in his room, but she refused to snoop in there while he wasn't around.

After a while, her mind got tired of trying to picture Danny and his wife living happily-ever-after in this house and found a window at the front of the house to watch the snow fall until he came back.

When his truck pulled in the drive, she watched him getting bags out of the cab with that same nervous expectancy of before, mixed with a strange domestic, warm feeling that she tried to push away fast. Danny was not interested in setting up house with her, and letting that thought breathe life for even a minute was way too dangerous.

"Watch yourself, Caity. This isn't a fairy tale. He's interested in the free sex you offered—nothing else."

She met him at the door and took the bags while he shook snow off his jacket and hung it up, then threw his boots into the box again, beside hers. She started to the kitchen with two of the bags when she felt his arm reached around her waist and haul her back against him.

"Wait up." He kissed her neck, sucked on her earlobe. "I missed you."

She giggled. "You did?"

She didn't care how many times she warned herself, she liked Danny. She liked not being alone for the moment, and she liked whatever this was that threatened to consume her like a slow burn.

He turned her in his arms, took the bags and placed them on the floor.

"Yeah, I did." His fingers skimmed the skin of her neck, slipped between the strands of hair and drew her even closer until his lips captured and sucked at hers. Her stomach tipped as she melted into the arms of her favorite person on the planet. At least for now, she silently warned herself.

His tongue pressed against hers, running

along the edge, enough to make her crazy with want again. The need to touch him came on her fast. She wanted to reach towards his jeans, but ran her fingers over his arms to his shoulders, then over his back. The feel of his skin as it gave to muscles intrigued her. She couldn't wait to see him naked, to feel his skin against hers.

Too soon, he pulled away with a lopsided grin and rubbed the back of his neck. "I bought ice cream."

She blinked a couple of times, tried to regain equilibrium and helped him to the kitchen with the groceries. Together, they unpacked them, though Caitlyn had no idea where anything went, so she placed her items on the bar for Danny to get when he was done with his own.

"I think it goes without saying that they did not have any Christmas dinners for two. Or twenty-two, for that matter. They were pretty picked over. But I did get a roasted chicken, and I bought a bag of potatoes. I had no idea what kind of gravy you liked, so I bought one of everything. Oh! And I found a copy of Miracle on 34th Street. I realize some station will probably play it tonight, but I didn't want to take any chance it..."

Danny had been so happy with all he'd accomplished and, truth be told, at the idea of this impromptu Christmas with Caitlyn, he was on a high and didn't notice at first when she became quiet. When he looked up to see why, his heart tumbled end over end until it landed in no way softly at the soles of his feet.

She had tears in her eyes, though she blinked furiously at them, and pressed both lips between her teeth in a valiant effort not to cry.

He didn't think twice about it but pulled her into his arms and held her. As he rubbed her back and whispered soothing words into her ear, he knew he never wanted to be anywhere else but right here with Caitlyn.

He'd never felt so damn protective of anyone in his life. When you grow up on your own, you learn early on to look out for yourself. He'd yet to meet anyone that made him want to slay dragons and chase away nightmares. Caity did that to him, though—that and so much more.

"I don't have anyone, anymore." She sniffled even as she pressed her cheek against his shoulder. "No one does nice things for me, or even thinks of me. With my friends, I'm the one who remembers birthdays and calls to make sure they're okay. No one thinks of me."

She pulled her head back, unfisted her hands from his shirt and pressed the palm of one against his cheek. It was cool, and he covered it with his own on instinct. *I want to take care of you, Caity.* But he didn't say it because he knew he wasn't capable of the job. Caity deserved so much more than he was. More than he could ever hope to be, and he'd be damned if he'd screw up her life by trying to be a part of it.

She kissed him. Long and slow and

unbearably sweet until his toes curled in his socks against the stone floor. He had to pull away. She had no idea what she did to him. Resting his forehead against hers, he ran his tongue over his lips and tasted her sweet essence still there.

"I wanted you to have a nice Christmas, Caity." He breathed deep, inhaling her scent, filling his lungs with it. "After we unpack, if you want, I have some Christmas stuff in the basement. It should be easy to get to, and..."

He hedged, not just because he didn't want her to cry again, but more because he'd done something that felt right at the time, and it left him vulnerable. A place he detested with all he was worth.

He took his hand from her waist and rubbed his neck with it. "The tree lot by the market had what was left, laying around with 'free' signs."

"You got us a tree?"

The disbelief mixed with childlike wonder in her eyes was everything he'd ever looked for his entire life. But what the hell was he supposed to do with it? She leapt into his arms this time, grabbed him around the neck and laughed with delight.

Oh, Caity. I always want to make you this happy.

If only I was capable.

****

Caitlyn nuzzled her nose against the warm spot on Danny's neck. They sat curled up on his sofa with chocolate chip cookies and a tub of whipped cream. Mugs of hot chocolate sat cooling on the coffee table, and they were almost at the part where the U.S. Post Office helped prove the existence of Santa Claus in her favorite Christmas movie of all time.

All in all, it had been a perfect Christmas. Danny and she had laughed and sang off key to carols while they worked together in the kitchen, whipping up mashed potatoes, some green beans he had in cans in the pantry and several cans of ready made crescent rolls to go with the chicken he bought.

Sure, it wasn't Christmas at the Waldorf, but it was possibly the nicest Christmas she'd ever had, and for someone who thought they'd avoid it altogether, it was especially wonderful. Now, she sat between his thighs as they stretched out on the sofa. Danny's arms wrapped around her body and kept her tugged close to him, not that she wanted to be anywhere else. A minute ago, she'd maneuvered to gain access to his neck. She pressed her face against the warm spot above the crook of his neck and inhaled the scent of gravy and cinnamon and musk.

She dipped her finger in the tub of cream and spread it in the curve, then licked and sucked the sweet cream and the taste of Danny into her mouth. He growled and laughed and tipped her back in the crook of his arm, then kissed her until she could barely breathe.

"Danny, I need you. Let me make love to you."

"Ah, sweetheart."

His head dipped. He bit her shoulder through the thin cotton fabric of her dress. She knew he wanted to wait, even understood why, but her hormones argued vehemently that now was far better than waiting. In her desperation, she lost whatever shyness she had left and pushed her hands up under his T-shirt. His skin was warm and soft, stretched taught over firm muscles.

Danny groaned but didn't stop her exploration. She moved her hands around his waist and up his chest, her fingers traveling through light chest hair until she found his nipples. She squeezed one but wanted her mouth on it. She wanted to suck on it and watch it harden the way hers did.

"Caity, sweetheart, stop." His tone was gentle even as it warned, but she didn't care.

"I want you, Danny. If you want to wait, you gotta give me something."

He groaned again, pushed her back onto the sofa and sat atop her thighs, one knee in the crease of the sofa, the other on the edge. He pulled his shirt over his head exposing himself. Caitlyn's mouth went dry, her breath deserted her and her heart stopped, she was sure of it. To say he was beautiful, probably wasn't right, but beautiful he was, at least as far as she was concerned.

Muscles and skin and flat brown nipples hidden under coarse black hair—she couldn't resist touching him. She ran her hands over his chest, circled his waist and ran them up his back. She sat up beneath him and brought her mouth within an inch of him before looking up into his hooded gaze. His mouth was pressed into a thin line, and she gathered he was feeling a lot like she was. She didn't waste another second because she knew he was giving her leeway he couldn't afford.

Her tongue boldly flicked his nipple once, but it wasn't anywhere near enough. She brushed her thumb over it. Already hard from her earlier touches, it stood erect and almost begged her to take it in her mouth. She licked it again, this time she was more direct and moved in a slower motion. Danny's breath hissed, his hands tightened on her forearms. She knew her time was running out, so she took the whole thing in her mouth, pressed it to the roof of her mouth and rubbed it with her tongue. Groaning as the movement turned her on and made her vulva pulse in needy bursts.

The rumble started low in his chest but was soon a controlled roar. He grabbed her head, framed her face in his hands and kissed her hard. His mouth ground on hers, his tongue plunged deep. Caitlyn felt her clit start to throb. She needed to come.

She wasn't an expert in that area—masturbation was not a natural fact of her life, the way it apparently was for Val. She'd masturbated a few times when she was a teen but felt awkward and guilty afterward, and she'd never seen what the big deal was and so had shied away. But that was definitely what she needed now. Only she didn't want her own hands between her legs, she wanted Danny's. His fingers, his tongue, his...

She became bold as she waded in deeper to the crazed, desperate pool of need that Danny's kisses and teasing were driving her to.

He kissed her hard and held her head in place as his tongue ran over hers and then explored her entire mouth. His bare chest mashed against her covered one, it wasn't right. Skin to skin. It was a necessity.

Caitlyn wriggled and squirmed until he stopped kissing her. Forehead to forehead, his harsh breath against her skin, he held her. She could feel his heart beating hard and fast and knew he wanted her at least as much as she needed him. She took his hand, guided it along her thighs. He groaned again, but she heard it for the sound of weakness it was and thrilled in it.

"I'm wet. Touch me and see how much I need you."

"Caity." The thready sound of his voice told her she was winning. Told her he was weakening.

"Please. It'll be okay, Danny. I promise."

He sat up again, ran his hands over his

head, through his hair. He stared down at her as if deciding. The DVD had long since ended and shut off, the only sounds now were the quiet hiss of gas flames, the wind blowing snow around outside, the mixed sounds of their harsh breathing and the rapid beating of their hearts.

Caitlyn sat up, slid the shoulders of her dress off. Danny stopped her. Both his hands covered hers, his eyes had lost their frenzy and softened to a dark grey in the firelight.

"I still intend to move slow, but I'll take care of you, Caity love."

He pushed her hands aside and slid the top of her dress off her shoulders. She helped him free her arms, and he pushed the top down around her waist. With only a thin bra to cover her, Caitlyn shivered with expectancy, his weight on her legs making her feel oddly secure. She leaned away from him to lay back against the sofa; moonlight drifted in the full length windows behind her and bathed them both in a soft glow. His naked chest was even more attractive in the faint light. She practically salivated at the thought of exploring his body.

Danny looked down at her with reverence. She'd never once in her life felt treasured before, but that was how he made her feel now. His fingers moved out to touch the peach lace that covered her breasts. The slowness of the movement spoke of how tentative he was, and maybe too, in a strange way, of how eager.

"Touch me, Danny."

She whispered her encouragement, his eyes flared, then his hand covered her. His other scooped behind her neck and brought her close enough to receive another kiss that scorched to her soul. He moaned into her mouth as his tongue swept through.

"Caity. My Caity. I need you so much. You have no idea. No idea how long I've needed."

She wanted to weep for how lost and alone he sounded in that moment. She got the distinct impression he spoke of so much more than physical need. She knew how desperate that need was by the rock solid length of him pressed up against her, evident even through the denim. She wondered if it were at all possible that the two loneliest people on the planet had somehow found each other on the most sacred night of the year.

She didn't answer, but held him closer, kissed him harder. She arched into his hand as her own need grew. The wetness between her thighs increased as did the throb. She adjusted her position enough that his groin pressed against her. Lord have mercy, how she needed him inside her.

Originally, when she'd set her mind on losing her virginity, it had been a decision made with her mind. It was a matter of fact that happened in every girl's life at one point. She figured if she got it over with, it would no longer be such a big deal in hers. Not once did she take into account that she could ever *want* it this much, and she was so glad she'd found this man.

She didn't even want to think about the experience of losing her virginity in the cold, calculated way she'd planned. She only wanted Danny.

His mouth suckled her neck, his palm pressed against her nipple, turning and twisting it, bringing it to a frantic peak. His other hand held her back firm, held her against him. When he brought his mouth away from hers, he sat back again, skimming his palms over the bare skin of her abdomen toward the front clasp on the lacy bra.

"God, you're beautiful."

Fingers trembling, Danny reached for the clasp. He couldn't remember another time a woman had made him this nervous, this excited or this hard either, for that matter. He flicked the clasp, moved with care when he pushed the soft lace to each side and bared her breasts to his view, his touch.

His stomach twisted and dropped, his heart stuttered. She was perfect. Her round, soft breasts were crowned with dusky peach nipples, already hard and pebbled.

"I'm going to lick you now, Caitlyn." He brought his head right to her breast and stopped. He blew on the nipple, and she shivered. He looked up into her gaze. "Then I'm going to suck on you."

They both swallowed at his erotic words of promise and firm tone. Danny framed one nipple with his hands, squeezed her breast gently, and licked the full length of her, from one edge of the areola over the nipple to the other edge. He moved slow and savored every ounce of flesh, tasted her and committed the flavor to memory.

He laved the tip again, blew on it and loved it when she squirmed beneath him, even though it made him crazy when she pressed her pussy against his cock. He knew she'd be so wet, by now dripping. If he dared take off her panties, his tongue would find her so hot and ready he'd probably come in his jeans.

Like he promised, he sucked the nipple between his lips, only the tip. He flicked it with his tongue several times, and ran his hands over the smooth skin of her waist, resting on her hips. He made the movement again and again until she cried out and clamped her hands down hard onto his shoulders. Her dainty nails biting into the skin.

"More, Danny. I need more."

He cupped the other breast, ran his thumb over the nipple, back and forth, then pinched it with measured strength while he sucked the first one deeper into his mouth. He sucked harder, and his passions would not abate. Instead he found them growing to dangerous proportions.

He wanted to touch her pussy. Wanted to slip his finger deep inside her, feel the walls of her sex close around him. The ache in his cock grew, intensified to the point of pain. If he didn't find release now on his own, he'd fuck her hard and long on his sofa right this very minute.

It was with great pain that he pulled his mouth away from her. His breath came hard and fast. He looked down at her nipple, glistening from where his mouth had been, and he felt the beginning contraction of an orgasm hit him.

"Oh fuck! Darlin' I'll be right back."

He did the only thing he could think of, he ran for the snow.

Chapter Four

Bracing himself against the cold, Danny slid out the side door and hid in the shadows of the house. After he ripped open his jeans and took his cock in hand, he pumped twice before his cum spurted from the tip. His low moan echoed in the stillness of the night, amplified by the fresh blanket of snow on the ground.

He pumped hard as his orgasm rolled on. Squeezing the shaft tight, he dreamed of Caity's pussy squeezing him, milking every last drop of cum into her beautiful body.

Christ!

He wanted to make a baby with her. He wanted to fill her womb with his seed and have it take root. Have their love...

Not love.

He wasn't good enough for anyone's love. He knew better than to even think it.

He had no idea how long he stood in the shadow of his house. He'd bought it for the sole purpose of filling it with love and babies, but he painfully reminded himself who he was, what he was capable of and what he was *not*.

He was freezing his ass off. He wondered if

his cock could get frostbite and shoved it back inside his jeans. He wasn't ready to go back inside. He couldn't face her. He knew she was aroused to a fever pitch, that she wanted him, but he couldn't give her what she really wanted, needed—a man to love her, treasure her. He wasn't that man, and she could do better. So he stood in the frozen night air in nothing but a pair of jeans and socks, trying to decide which was worse, death from hypothermia or facing Caity.

It was a harder decision than he ever could have believed.

****

Caitlyn sat up on the grey sofa she was becoming emotionally attached to in a mild state of shock.

Did the man just run *from me?*

What was so inherently wrong with her that made guys run? Okay, so this was the first one to do that, but Don had told her she was an emotional black hole of need, or words to that effect. He told her no one would ever be able to meet all her needs, and she'd be better off to castrate him than let him try and fail over and over again.

The first tear slipped down her cheek. She shoved her arms inside her dress and ran for the door, thrust on her boots and coat and ran to her car without even a glimpse back at her dead dream.

Merry Christmas, Caity.

****

Caitlyn spent the next two days in bed. She lost all interest in the holiday, her job, her friends, everything—especially her New Year's resolution. She couldn't go through that again, not ever. So, doomed to a life as a virgin, she lay in her bed and wallowed in self-pity and depression. She didn't answer her phone, didn't answer the door—though she had looked through the peek hole. The first time it was Naomi, the second time Mrs. Schuster from down the hall. And she did not think about tall, muscular bartenders with soft hair that curled at their collars and hands that should have been insured for the magic they could bring a girl.

And she refused to even *think* about his tongue.

Well, that was if she thought about him at all, which she absolutely would not.

She ate the equivalent of two gallons of Hagen Dasz vanilla Swiss almond, three dozen Christmas cookies and a rum-soaked fruitcake that had been delivered to her house by mistake. Originally she'd planned to take it back, but... oh well.

In her ratty old bathrobe and rabbit slippers she watched old love stories, tear jerkers and reality television until she thought she might puke.

Where exactly did all those people come from that aren't afraid to show all of America how pathetic they are?

Not that she wasn't outright pathetic herself, but she wasn't about to go on some talk show for an episode entitled, *Women So Pathetic They Can't Even Give It Away*, and show all America the proof.

She was fat, she was sick to her stomach from too much sugar and rum, and she was beginning to smell.

Oh well.

She snuggled deeper into the thrift store armchair and took a nap. Jerry Springer didn't start until three.

****

Danny was going crazy. He had no idea how to find his Caity. He'd been too hormonally challenged to get a phone number, her friends hadn't been in. Hell, he had no way to even know if they were regulars or not, since his usual routine didn't include much time spent out front.

The week between Christmas and New Year's was the worst time of the year for him. Too many bad memories. Memories of dreams that never came true, and worse, memories of a frosty night three days after Christmas when the police called to have him come and ID Margo's body.

He shivered even now from the memory. The coldness it left etched on his heart never left him. It was like living a nightmare—one where you tried to outrun the bad guy but just knew you never would. Still, you ran and ran, terror clawing at your insides until you felt sick. He felt sick from December first to mid-February, and his usual remedy for dealing with the holidays was to turn into a sadistic workaholic.

No job was too hard, boring or beneath him. He'd do anything to keep from being reminded that Margo chose death over being married to him. This year, however, he wished he hadn't logged himself down with so much. He could barely get away for an hour and that wasn't enough time to find her.

He'd been to the graveyard twice everyday, but he never saw her, and there weren't any fresh flowers in the vases. He went by the coffee shop, but considered that a long shot at best to begin with. Hell, he'd even Googled her. And he had prayed in every available second that somehow she'd come back to him.

Pathetic, but it was all he knew to do.

****

"I'm so glad you agreed to come out with us tonight, honey."

Naomi gave her a funny squeeze, not quite a hug, more of a hand shake with both hands to her forearms. Warm and fuzzy it wasn't, but then again, maybe that was her too-needy persona talking. She grunted a response, not at all convinced *she* was glad she'd come out with them tonight.

Val pulled a bottle of vodka from her purse and handed it to her. "Here. The holidays always seem brighter if you're a little toasted."

She eyed the bottle, eyed Val, then downed a fourth of the bottle in one gulp and choked when Naomi pulled it away.

"Knock it off, Val. She doesn't need your meddling now."

Val rolled her eyes with a dramatic air, switched her weight from one foot to the other, and gave a very unladylike sound of disbelief, somewhere between a snort and chuckle. "And what she needs is you and your uptight prissy interference?"

"Well, she sure the hell—"

"Enough!" Caitlyn raised both arms in the air as she snuck between them, then grabbed the bottle of vodka and took another swig. "What I need is a good fuck. And New Year's Eve is just the time to do it. If I can't find a willing guy tonight, shoot me in the head tomorrow, all right?"

"All right." Valerie's voice was deadpan as she took the vodka back. She looked askance at how much Caitlyn had taken.

"Caitlyn!" Naomi, on the other hand, was her usual high-strung control-freak self.

God, how Caitlyn loved both of them. Without warning, she grabbed both into a gregarious group hug. Neither friend "did" hugs, but this was New Year's, and Caitlyn decided no one was bringing her down tonight.

"I love you guys." She gave them each kisses on the cheek, which she thought they both seemed more appalled than pleased with. "Now let's go get laid!"

****

Danny prayed to God this would work. He was out of time and out of ideas. If Caitlyn had gone back to her original plan to lose her virginity by the stroke of midnight...well, he didn't even want to think about it. Caitlyn was his, and no other guy better even think of putting his hands on her or he'd fucking tear the bastard limb from limb.

He ran his hands through his hair, a maneuver that was a blatant show of the frustration he felt. It had been a long week. A week of soul-searching and self-discovery along with a long week of slowly losing whatever sanity he had left.

He drew a breath deep into his lungs. It was do or die time, because for whatever reason, Caitlyn was different. He *knew* deep down that if he didn't take the chance—swing at the ball and not worry about striking out—he'd regret it until the day he died.

Caity was the one for him. He and Margo had been a bad fit from the start. He had his head in the clouds and hadn't realized until it was too late that she had needs there was no way in hell he could ever meet. He was still Danny, though he promised to work on all his idiosyncrasies and be whatever she needed him to be, but bottom line, Caity wasn't Margo.

Caity was bright and awkward and cheery,

and most of all—alive. She was more alive than Margo had ever been. All he had to do was look at Caity, and he saw it, her joy. It burned bright in her eyes and in her soul. She'd save him from the blackness, and he'd save her right back. From the loneliness, the fear of never fitting in or finding her way in life and anything else she needed saving from.

He'd give her that picket fence, a whole litter of puppies, babies and anything else she wanted. He'd be her damn white knight in shining armor from this day forth, and this time, it would be enough. This time he'd do it right. Together, Caity and he would find their way and life would be blessed.

All he had to do was find her.

He checked his watch for the millionth time. If she'd found someone to replace him on her New Year's quest, that gave him just over four hours to find her and convince her to trust him again. And this time...*fuck going slow.*

****

After shuffling through a fresh layer of snow in the parking lot, the girls crammed into the rowdy New Year's Eve crowd down at the moose lodge. Caitlyn ignored her frozen toes as she gave her coat to the check girl. Looking around, she thought there were enough examples of raw machismo here to do the deed. She just had to find one that made her...well, not feel what Danny did. She didn't think anyone would do that, but at least one that made her feel

71

something. Made her a little wet between the thighs, if nothing else.

She'd forgone panties tonight and chosen a red velvet dress, short and tight and showing enough cleavage to get the message across—*I'm a sure thing.* She also hoped maybe she could find some guy who wouldn't be opposed to just doing it up against a wall somewhere. The lack of panties would aid in the fast fuck she was looking for.

It no longer mattered to her how long it took or how suave the guy was. She just didn't want to be a virgin anymore. She was tired of laughing at jokes she didn't understand, blinking with wide-eyed innocence pretty much every time Val opened her mouth, and she was really tired of guys who got that deer-in-the-headlights look anytime she braved telling them about her virginal state.

As the night progressed, she found a couple of possibilities. She even went so far as to let them nibble on her neck. One even got to feel her up, though Caitlyn hadn't actually *let* him, it sort of just happened. Anyway, that was in the past and right now she had her eye on a blond cutie with dimples working as the DJ for tonight's festivities.

He didn't have Danny's biceps, or his smile, or his stormy grey-blue eyes, or his...*Stop that!*

She sighed, straightened her spine along with her resolve, reminded herself that Danny did *not* want her, and started towards the DJ booth.

The big screen TV was turned up now, tuned into the local station's New Year's broadcast which would go live to NYC and the ball drop at midnight. With the DJ on break, this was her opportunity. It looked like he was taking requests. Caitlyn had a request. She tugged down her dress, flipped back her hair, which she'd worn down and even curled, and blotted her cherry lip gloss covered lips.

Going in.

"This is Kelley Clarkson." Obnoxious giggle. As Caitlyn crossed the floor, she mouthed with the reporter her next words, "*Not* the pop star."

Caitlyn hated that bleach-blonde insipid reporter on channel twelve. She tried to block out the woman's voice and concentrate on blond fuck buddy across the dance floor.

If she stopped and paid any attention to herself, she would have hated the way her mind was working lately, and her mouth right along with it. She wasn't raised to speak that way, or even think that way, and to be honest, it didn't feel natural. She pushed out with purpose all the sweet naïve thinking that had gotten her nowhere all these years and replaced it with Val's persona. Her mother was surely tossing in her grave.

"Tonight being New Year's, we here at channel twelve hope you stay safe and don't drink and drive."

Caitlyn rolled her eyes, not at the

sentiment, she just really didn't like Kelley Clarkson, *not* the pop star. Which Caitlyn was sure the blonde bimbo had legally changed her full name to.

"Okay, we've got one hour to New Year's, and with me tonight is owner of The Cherry Blossom Cantina on First Street across from Pop's Auto Repair. Hell of a margarita you guys serve, Danny."

Caitlyn froze in her steps. The reporter's obnoxious giggle ran the length of her spine like shards of glass. She turned to the big screen with great amounts of trepidation. She wasn't certain she could take seeing him after all that had happened. She'd driven by his house twice, because she wanted to apologize for how she'd run out on him, but he hadn't been home. She never perked up the courage to go by the cantina.

Naomi's fingers squeezed her shoulders, but she didn't take her eyes from the screen as Danny came into view. "Thanks, Kelley."

He was heart-stoppingly beautiful in his tux. His hair seemed thicker, glossier and even though it looked like he was overdue for a cut, she hoped he wouldn't. She still remembered how those strands curled at his neck and how they felt between her fingers. It was silly, but she'd feel the loss if he cut them.

He took the mike from Kelley, and the camera zoomed in on him. Caitlyn wanted to cry. Why couldn't he have felt for her what she'd felt for him? It would have been so perfect between them. Oh, not that she thought he was perfect, and God knew she wasn't, but together, they would have found their own version of perfection.

Together, they would have been whole in a way she would never be alone. Oh, that wasn't to say she needed a man to be a whole functioning member of society, it was just that she'd been created with a Danny-shaped hole inside her, and without him, she wouldn't be...complete.

"I hope everyone in the listening area is having a good night, keeping safe and all that. I'm here tonight with an announcement that I sincerely hope you all will pay attention to and help me out with a little problem I've got going on in my personal life."

He shifted the mike to his other hand, licked his lips and looked so nervous Caitlyn felt her heart's wrap on the man grow more solid.

"You see, I've met a woman. The perfect woman, really, but I did something stupid and scared her off. I've looked all over the place for her, but...well, suffice it to say, I'm the world's biggest a...uh, idiot."

He smiled at his faux pas, and Caitlyn thought his cheeks pinked a bit. She leaned forward as if she could reach through the screen and touch him, hold him close and make everything okay again.

"Caity, sweetheart. If you're listening, I'm so

sorry. And if you give me another chance, I won't even think the word slow if that's what you want." His voice trembled, and she saw the turmoil flash in his eyes as the camera rolled in close. "Please, come back to me, honey."

The first tear slipped without warning, and her feet tried to move of their own accord, but she stayed them. Uncertainty barreled through and left her confused. She longed for him in a way she knew was special and that she would never feel for another man, but was he that sure about her? Because if he wasn't, well, she wasn't up for another ride on the merry-go-round.

She didn't mind the roller coasters—ups and downs and moments that scare the life out of you, but when the ride ended you'd experienced something. The merry-go-round didn't even have a separate exit point. You got off at exactly the same point you got on.

"And this is for the rest of you." She refocused on the man and his plea. "In case she doesn't see this, or can't trust me, her name's Caitlyn. Now, I'm not giving you her last name on account of she deserves her privacy, and she isn't listed with the phone company, anyway. God knows, I tried that one fifty times." He smiled and gave a shaky wave. "Hi, Phoebe. Sorry about that by the way. Nice people at the phone company."

Caitlyn laughed as he rubbed the back of his neck. What the heck had he done to the poor phone operator? And had he really tried to find her? She was unlisted, like he said. Even if the number was listed, the phone was still in her mother's name. She'd tried to change it, but according to the phone company, Caitlyn Monson didn't exist. It seemed the last few years she hadn't been living, only taking care of her mom, and her identity was lost.

"Anyway, my Caity's about this tall..." he held his hand flat with his chin. "Has dark blonde hair I think comes to about here, uh, well about here." He moved his hand level with his chest. Caitlyn smothered a giggle. "She's the sweetest girl in the whole world with big green eyes and the cutest little overbite. If any of you know her and can convince her to come talk with me, or you know where I can find her..."

He shuffled his weight to the other foot again and rubbed his fingers over one eye. He looked tired, and she wished she could hold his head in her lap and let him sleep.

"Well, dinner for you and three of your friends every week for life at the Cherry Blossom." He looked up a bit sheepish. "Sorry if you hate the place, it's the best I've got to offer. I want another shot with my Caity. Please help me."

The hush that had fallen around her was broken by collective aw's, oh's and other generic sighs. Caitlyn didn't know what to think. She stared into his grey-blue eyes as if he were standing there in front of her.

"I'll be here at the station till midnight.

After that, well, she knows where I live. I'll wait up for you, Caity." He handed the mike back, and it picked up a soft, "Thank you, Kelley."

Then the blonde bimbo with the fake smile and faker boobs was back on screen all soft and gushy and putting her hands all over Danny. Caitlyn didn't like it, and she didn't like how she wanted to scratch her eyes out and pull that fake blonde weave right off her head.

"Aw, Danny, that's the sweetest thing I've ever heard. If your Caity's listening and won't give you another chance, I know the girls'll be lining up around the block to help you over your heartache." Yet another obnoxious giggle that softened into a purr sound. "Me included, sugar. Now, we're about to check in with Mike out at Bozane's. How's the party heating up over there, Mike?"

Caitlyn felt as if the world had collapsed in on top of her. She wanted nothing more than to run to that station and into Danny's arms. She knew exactly where the station was, too, and if they hurried, she could still be de-virginized by New Year's.

She let out a slow breath. Her heart beat so fast she bet she could keep time with hummingbird wings.

"What are you gonna do, honey?"

Caitlyn looked up and caught Naomi's gaze.

She wanted to die this week. She'd stayed in bed and ate herself sick, and nothing more than a teenage make-out session had gone on between them. If she slept with him, let him take her virginity, how would she ever survive losing him then?

"I don't know."

****

Danny paced the concrete floor of the studio. Kelley Clarkson—*not* the pop star—was doing another live check-in with one of the three reporters in the field tonight. Thank God, because when she wasn't, she was looking at him like he was roast lamb steaming on a platter surrounded by dollops of fresh cream and a few emeralds.

He cursed under his breath. The thought of emeralds made him think of Caitlyn's eyes, and the thought of cream took his mind right back to his night with Caitlyn and his cock right back to extra hard. He didn't know whether she'd show tonight or not, but his hopes were up. Unless she was at a private party somewhere, it was quite likely she'd seen his plea. Channel twelve had the largest viewing public on a regular night, and tonight they had the exclusive feed of NYC's legendary ball drop, so every tavern, lodge and restaurant with a television would be tuned in.

It didn't hurt that they had already replayed his moment of infamy twice after a boatload of calls came into the station with requests to see the lovesick fool again.

Okay, so maybe they hadn't referred to him that way, but it was certainly what he thought of himself. He couldn't help it, he was head-over-ass for the girl, and his gut told him she'd seen it. Now the question remained, would she show?

Chapter Five

Five...Four...

Danny held his breath. She hadn't shown, but maybe. It wasn't midnight yet. He couldn't give up even with that small voice deep inside him insisting she wasn't coming.

Three...

His heart refused to give up. Wouldn't admit defeat. He craned his neck to look down the long hallway, then out the large bank of windows into the parking lot.

Two...

No headlights of approaching cars, no bodies bustling in the cold towards the warmth and shelter the building offered. Nothing. But she'd come.

One.

She has to come. That's how it works in all the fairy tales.

Happy New Year!

He closed his eyes.

This wasn't a fairy tale.

No, what he and Caitlyn shared had been the single best day of his life, but like everything else, it hadn't lasted.

He pulled his tie loose, flexed his hands and grabbed his jacket from over a nearby chair. He walked in a haze from the channel twelve offices, while its employees celebrated the New Year and the hope for new beginnings everyone always believed it held.

Everyone but him. Danny didn't want to hold onto hope for anything anymore.

He wasn't sure how he'd traversed the myriad of hallways and corridors and wound up outside by his truck, but the cold air, with its January wind cutting across the vast space, hit him hard, left his skin burning and brought him to his senses.

"God damn you, loser!"

He swiped an armful of snow off the hood of his truck. Hadn't he learned anything? Hadn't he learned at the age of six that parents leave? At ten that they can and do die? Hadn't he learned at twelve that you couldn't trust kids who said they were your friend? That they'd sure as shit stab you in the back the second you looked away?

At thirteen, fifteen and sixteen he'd learned that foster parents lie and were more interested in their monthly checks and biological children than in some mutt they'd taken in. And the kicker, at twenty-four he learned he was a shit for a husband. In fact, he was so bad that the divorce papers weren't enough for her. Three days after Christmas, Margo took so many damn pills she'd made sure she would never have to lay eyes on him again.

"How many times did she tell you what a loser you were?"

How many times when he'd tried to make love to her, had she lain there and looked at the ceiling? How many times had she cried herself to sleep, wishing she hadn't married him?

Pain ripped through him as real as a blade slicing into every inch of skin, every shred of muscle, and right down to his soul. Tears welled in his eyes, a lump in his throat. He climbed in the cab and put the keys in the ignition.

He'd tried so hard to make something of himself. Had worked his ass off to prove to them all that he was worth more than any of them thought. If one damn thing had turned out right, he could have stood up to every critic he'd ever faced and laughed, but in the end they'd been right. Every person who'd ever told him he'd never make it in this world. Everyone who'd told him he didn't have what it took to make something of himself. They'd all been right. Every damn one.

He wasn't worth the air he breathed, and for a moment, he thought maybe Margo had been the smart one for getting out. Not of the marriage, but out of this damn, fucking thing called life.

****

The headlights of his truck made the wide half-circle from street to house as he swung it into the drive. The house was dark. He half

83

laughed. It was irony at its finest.

"Dark like my heart." He swung his arms wide, made a circle, head back shouting at the heavens. "Dark like my future!"

He laughed with derision as he stuck his keys in the lock, the sound of tumblers turned, the creaky door sounded when it swung open. He tossed his boots into the box without looking, but left his jacket on and went straight for the Jim Beam.

He hadn't remembered leaving the fire on.

"Good job, shit-for-brains. Next you'll burn down your own god damned house."

He went to the wood and marble bar he hardly ever used and poured himself a tumbler full of the dark liquid. His heart ached. His head might as well ache, because he intended to get shit-faced tonight.

As he neared the sofa, he tripped over his own feet and about dropped the glass. He closed his eyes tight. Opened them. Closed them again.

"God, tell me I'm not fuckin' nuts on top of everything else. Sweetheart, tell me that's you."

****

Caitlyn sat up on one elbow, the white chiffon gown slipped over her body in an arousing caress. "I couldn't bear to show up at the station. Okay, truth, I was scared." She laughed. "Open your eyes."

He did, slowly.

"Danny, I was a mess all week. I'm scared of how I'll feel when you don't want me anymore, but I'm more scared of not having this experience with you."

He hadn't moved a step since he first saw her. Even now, as he reached to put his glass on the table, his feet stayed glued to the carpet.

"Danny? Tell me its going to be okay."

With two steps he covered the distance between them, dropped to his knees, and she was back in his arms—the only place in the world she ever wanted to be.

"Love me, Danny. Make me a woman tonight."

He stood, cradled her head in his palms, his thumbs gently grazing her face. "You missed your deadline."

She shrugged. "I did."

He breathed deep. Caitlyn did the same, loving the scent of musk and snow and pine on his jacket and skin. He was still cold from being outside, and the cool touch on her heated flesh caused her nipples to harden and tiny goosebumps to break out everywhere else. But nothing mattered so long as Danny would have her.

"You want to be a woman?"

"I want you to teach me. Show me everything."

He gave her a slow and tender kiss, so deep it reached into her soul and set fire to it. His hands climbed up the outside of her slight negligee, pressing her closer. "The sight of you in this damn near killed me, sweetheart."

"I didn't want "go slow" to be an option."

He laughed hard, his eyes dilated as he took her in, head to foot.

"Never again, sweetheart." He framed her face again, stared deep into her eyes and growled. "Tonight, we fuck like rabbits, baby."

The erotic promise sent a thrill to her core and laughter bubbled to the surface. Danny pressed her to the sofa. "First thing tomorrow…" One side of his mouth crept up in a wicked lopsided grin. "Well, maybe not *first* thing, but I'm buying a new bed. Tonight the sofas will have to do. I'm not going to love you in the bed I shared with Margo. Can you understand that?"

She touched his cheek in a tender gesture and hoped to assure him that nothing else mattered. She didn't care about the bed, or his reasons, she only wanted to be with him. Her Danny had a lot of pain and a lot of secrets. She prayed one day he'd share them with her, but for now, his touch, his kiss, was all she needed.

"I love these sofas. Some of the best moments of my life occurred on them."

He kissed her slow and soft, wet and deep. "Prepare for another one, sweetheart."

His hand ran along the outside of her thigh until it reached the hem of her gown. He circled her ankle, scooted towards her feet and held one up. Caitlyn's gaze locked on his as he sucked each of her toes. Electric surges zipped along her synapses, landing dead center on her clit. She clenched involuntarily in response. Her breath locked in her chest, effectively stifling the girlish giggle on her lips. He kissed the soles of her feet and the insides of her ankles as if they were precious and Caitlyn knew she was in for far more than just sex. Tonight would change her for the rest of her life.

His fingers slid the length of her thighs, and he separated them before he slid between. He looked up with a heated gleam in eyes that were filled with illicit promises, eyes that held so much desire. The effect churned up her own internal flame until she almost couldn't breathe.

"Has anyone ever made you come before, sweetheart?"

She shook her head, words beyond her at this point. His grin sent those flames licking up the inside of her thighs and straight into her womb. She felt his breath on her slick folds and waited, knowing what he was about to do but with no way to prepare for it. He glanced up to find her watching him with desperate intensity. Gaze locked with hers, he blew on the lips of her labia. Soaked with her own juices and so hot she thought she might burst into flames, she felt her internal muscles clench in response to his erotic overtures.

He breathed deep. "I love your scent. It drives me crazy." He licked her, slow and long, she nearly shot off the sofa.

"Oh my lord!"

He growled. "And your taste..."

Caitlyn swallowed and tried to stay still as

he licked her, sucked her clit and slid one finger inside her. "Good God, Danny. Does it always feel like this?"

He smiled. She could feel it against her intimately.

"I wouldn't know, sweetheart. I don't have a pussy of my own."

He laughed, and then she swore his tongue slipped inside her. She cried out and slapped a hand over her mouth.

"Honey, you go ahead and make noise. That's the kinda thing makes a guy beat his chest. Nothing would turn me on more than to hear you scream when I make you come."

He punctuated his sentence with one long lick and a quick nip on her clit.

"Heaven help me, I'm gonna come now!"

"I think heaven already outdid itself tonight by bringing you here. Don't overtax it."

She laughed and then started to cry as the wave built inside her and she realized it wasn't always this good. It would never have been this good with anyone else. She didn't have to be an experienced woman to know this was different. Everything she felt—from the physical sensation to the emotional ones—was all because, for whatever reason, she'd given her heart to Danny.

"I love you, Danny."

She said it on a whisper, and hoped he hadn't heard her. It was too much, but she had to say it. Now that she'd recognized them, the words wouldn't stay put no matter how hard she tried.

His fingers picked up speed as they slid in and out of her. She flexed and arched without the power to stop it. She writhed and brought herself closer, rubbing herself on his face while he devoured her voraciously. She couldn't hold back any longer. It was like she stood at the top of a waterfall, ready to dive in but too terrified to actually make the leap. Finally, thank God, she was pushed and had no choice but to tumble over the edge into heaven. The trip was spectacular.

She shook and cried and felt completely stupid when the last of her tremors subsided. Danny scooted up beside her, held her close and kissed her temple, eyes, and lips. She tasted herself on him, caught her scent on his breath and thought it should have grossed her out, but instead, it made her feel like she belonged to him...and always would.

Danny felt as if half his brain cells had exploded right along with Caity. He tried to focus on her, on her pleasure alone. This was her first time, and he wanted it to be amazing and a moment she'd always remember.

His gut cramped at the thought of her moving on, being with other men. He wanted to imprint himself on her at a molecular level so no matter where she went or who she was with, no one would ever compare to him.

No, it wasn't fair, but that's what she'd done

to him. With her little giggles, her soft warm pussy and her adorable little overbite. He'd never love another woman the way he loved Caitlyn, and he was tired of denying it.

He kissed her, slow and deep with all the longing in his heart on raw display. Then he pulled away and began to remove his clothing. She followed his lead, sat up and slipped the flimsy negligee over her head and left him breathless.

He would love her tonight until the sun came up. Until he couldn't move, and he'd love her like he'd never done before. He'd give to her all that he was, tonight he wouldn't hold back. He'd give it all to his Caity, and if in the morning she walked away, he'd always have this one night to remember perfection.

I love you, Caity.

He grabbed the condom from his jeans. Already rock hard, his cock weeping pre-cum from the tip, he moved to sheath himself. Caitlyn held out her hand, a soft, "Wait," on her lips.

"What is it darlin'? 'Cause if I don't get inside you soon..."

"I want to taste you."

Holy shit!

His cock jumped and pushed out more salty fluid. When her finger slid over it, her eyes wide with fascination, it took all he had not to come all over her. She traced back and forth over the tip, then met his gaze and sucked the finger slowly into her mouth.

Cherry Blossom inventory. Beer, fifty seven kegs. Tequila, twelve bottles...

It was the only way.

"It's salty."

He groaned so deep and so long he sounded more animal than human.

"Can I put it in my mouth? Can I lick it?"

"No," he ground out between clenched teeth, his jaw so tight a muscle ticked within it. "It's not that I wouldn't love to indulge your every whim, particularly where my cock is concerned, but I swear darlin' if you even look at it again, I'm gonna come."

Her eyes got so big he feared her corneas might pop out. He laughed. He couldn't help himself. "Honey, it's okay. It's not gonna attack you."

She shook her head, blonde curls bounced around her face. *God, she's stunning.*

"It's not that." She reached for him again but pulled back at the last minute. If he didn't get the damn condom on soon... "Cock? That's what you call it?"

The laughter stuck in his throat, and he sheathed himself fast. "Yeah, darlin'."

She swallowed hard, and a blush crept up her cheeks. "And you called my, uh..." She dropped her voice to a whisper as if there were someone else in the room. "Pussy?"

Shoving her back on the sofa, he knelt between her thighs and slipped a finger deep inside her. Not that he didn't already know she was wet. He just needed to make one more check before he rammed his raging hard-on into her.

"Sweetheart, could we have this conversation a little later?"

He nudged her opening with his cock, pushed gently. Her pussy welcomed him straight away. He nearly wept.

"Oh, sure." Her voice sounded strained. "It's just that my mom always called everything by very clinical terms, and so I'm not real used to..." Her voice trailed off as he moved to cover her mouth with his.

He kissed her until she melted then pushed deeper inside her while she was distracted. She tensed, and her pussy tightened around him. He knew she had to be nervous so he moved his mouth lower, sucked in one tight bud of a nipple and rolled it on his tongue until she purred for him and opened the rest of the way.

"This part might hurt a bit, darlin'. I swear to God I'll be gentle."

She nodded, and he kissed her again until she relaxed. The price of heaven was bringing her pain, and he hated it. He hoped the band-aid theory worked with virginity as well. He wrapped his arms under her knees, pulled them up and pushed them back towards her body, opening her wider, then thrust past the barrier, fast.

She tensed beneath him again. He froze,

then sucked on the curve of her neck as his fingers played with her nipple. A moment later, her hands wound around his neck and into his hair. Her pussy muscles grabbed him to the point he had to hold back a moan. Tender emotions overwhelmed him like never before. He kissed her forehead, her nose, her lips, her chin.

I love you, Caity mine.

Not yours. Remember Margo.

The thought sickened him, but he shoved it away, picking up a quick rhythm, sliding in and out of her tight passage. Each pass brought him closer to the brink and soon he realized she wasn't going to climax again from his internal thrusts alone.

He pulled out.

She moaned her displeasure, and he kissed her hard.

"Turn over, love. I want you to come around my cock, and you're not going to unless I touch you."

She gave him a wide eyed doe look but flipped over, he put an arm around her waist and positioned her properly. The view about did him in. Her pink wet pussy in clear view, he wanted to suck on it again, lick it until she screamed. He gave in to temptation and ran his tongue over the length of her once, twice over her clit. When she yelped and looked over her shoulder, he met her shocked gaze with a wicked manifestation of his own. She was the perfect picture of sex—part innocent, part wanton—and all his.

He plunged back inside her and made quick work to regain the right rhythm. This time he was able to reach around and work her clit at the same time. When he stopped to think of all the positions and all the ways he planned to have her, he shook from the anticipation.

Her pussy grabbed him tighter, and her spasms started.

"Hang on baby, you're about to come again."

Her little yelps and squeals were so enticing, he couldn't imagine the day he'd ever have enough of her.

"Oh! Oh! Danny!"

"I know, baby. Come hard for me, sweetheart."

Her pussy clenched him. She was tight and wet and a dream come true. He started to come, his legs trembled from the power of his orgasm, and he feared for a minute he wouldn't be able to remain upright. He braced one arm against the back of the sofa, biting back his howl. As her orgasm started to wane, he slowed his touch and thrust into her a few more times until she'd milked him dry.

She fell on her stomach, pulling herself away from him. He would have laughed if he'd had the strength. As it was, it took all his concerted effort not to fall on top of her. He squeezed in beside her and pulled her body close to his. His hand came to rest protectively over one breast.

Their mingled breath filled the space around them as their sweat-sheened bodies started to cool. Danny grabbed the wool throw from the back of the sofa and covered them both. He kissed her head and pulled her as close as he could get her and swore as she fell into sleep she muttered, "I love you, Danny."

Chapter Six

Danny woke to the delicious smell of bacon and eggs and the empty feeling of being alone. Sprawled on his stomach, one arm hung off the edge of the sofa, his hand brushing the carpet. For a time he lay still with his eyes closed, breathing in the faint scent of her still on his skin and wondered if the ghost feel of her arms wrapped around him was permanent.

He'd tried to restrain himself last night, knew he had to take it easy with her, but he'd made love to her twice more through the night, and each time she stole more and more of his soul and he didn't give a damn.

His cock started to lengthen, his body's hunger changing from a need for sustenance to a need for Caity.

Once his eyes opened, it took less than a second to see her. She looked so perfect in his kitchen, wearing his tuxedo shirt from last night with the sleeves folded to her elbows. He turned to his side and propped his head on his hand to better watch her as she leaned over a pot on the stove and gently stirred its ingredients with a wooden spoon. If this wasn't heaven, Danny had no idea what was.

She was so *right*.

Right in his house, in his shirt, in his bed.

Just right for his life.

He pushed the thought away and grabbed for his pants.

Caitlyn couldn't stop the smile from blooming as Danny walked across the floor towards her. He had a definite gleam in his eyes she was learning to recognize. She grew wet and achy again, and her breaths became shallow with desire.

Last night had been so much more than she ever imagined. She knew in part it was because she was so in love with him. She'd spent half the morning pondering that.

She'd waken at some point when Danny stirred. The sofa was wonderful, but not quite big enough for two adults to sleep on comfortably together. Since the sun had cracked the horizon already, she decided not to go back to sleep, but to get up and make them breakfast. For a while, though, she just lay there in his arms. As she watched him sleep, she felt the warm brush of air across her cheek every time he exhaled and just reveled in the new found glow of being a woman.

How could you love someone you really didn't know at all? There was simply no other way to describe how she felt, though. It wasn't lust, it wasn't infatuation. It was stay-with-me-forever-and-be-my-other-half love.

Mom was right. You just know.

"Morning, sweetheart." His hands skimmed her waist and pulled her close. He brushed back her hair that had lost its curl and gained a whole lot of knots over the course of the night. "You feel okay?"

She averted her eyes, feeling her cheeks heat as she tried not to think about everything that had transpired between them last night and how wanton she'd become. She gave him a slight nod as she drowned in her own embarrassment and felt even sillier for feeling that way after the degree of intimacy they'd shared.

He tucked his fingers under her chin and pulled her gaze back to his. "Not too sore?"

She was sore in places she never even thought about, but not *too* sore. Not enough to not want to do it again right after breakfast. She nodded, reached around him and turned off the two burners she was working with.

"Breakfast smells wonderful." He placed a soft kiss on her lips, not too intimate, as if he was afraid he'd ignite passions that wouldn't wait. "I have a hot tub on the back deck. It'll help with whatever is sore. Maybe after breakfast, we could take a dip."

"I don't have a suit."

His eyes flashed with primal heat that left her breath frozen in her lungs. "You won't need one, sweetheart."

Her eyes roamed his chest, and she wanted

to take one of his nipples into her mouth. "I'm frying bacon, you know. It's not the safest place to be topless."

Her words were dreadfully breathy. She reached out and touched the flat surface of his abdomen. He shivered.

"It's turkey bacon, darlin', there's not enough fat on that to splatter past the pan." He mimicked her movements; his fingers wormed their way between the buttons of the shirt she wore. "You do know there is nothing more sexy than the woman you loved all night wearing your shirt, don't you?"

That breathy little giggle tried to get out again, but when she locked gazes with him, it died in her throat.

"I hadn't, actually." She gave a miniscule shrug. "I've never actually loved a woman before, but I could probably get Val on board so I could find out."

With a growl, he pulled her hard against his chest. Caitlyn found her feet now hung in mid air and wrapped her legs around him. Her bare pussy rubbed against the coarse fabric of his pants. She moaned wanting more, wanting him—all of him.

His mouth devoured her as if last night had never happened and he hadn't seen her for months. His tongue danced and mated with hers, fought for supremacy and she let him win, only to win herself when he sucked it into his mouth.

His hands moved down her back to cup her bottom, his fingers kneading her flesh as he pulled her higher and closer. One hand disappeared as he grabbed for a condom and unzipped. How he ever managed it with only one hand she'd never know, but the next thing she felt was her back pressed up against the fridge and his stiff cock against her opening.

"Now, Danny. Hurry!" She tilted her hips, enticing him in further and groaned when he started to slide deep inside her. "I love this."

His deep laugh rumbled in his chest, and he bit her neck and shoulder and hugged her tight as his hips rocked out a rhythm against her poor slightly abused body. She smiled as the intimate and frenetic energy grabbed hold of her.

"Christ, honey, not half as much as I do, I assure you."

She'd discovered last night that her body only responded to his thrusts in certain positions. This hadn't been one they tried then, but it was working for her big time. With every thrust, his cock grazed her pussy walls and brought her closer to climax.

She did her best to match his rhythm, but with her body in a crazy frenzy of want and blazing desire, she felt like she was messing him up more than helping. She felt like an animal, raw and needy.

"Baby, I'm gonna come."

She sensed in his tone that he was trying to wait for her. She held on tight, pressed her face into his neck and whispered, "Come for me, then."

His body went rigid, the muscles throughout his body tensing with the onslaught of his orgasm. Somehow he had the presence of mind to reach between them and touch her clit. Once was enough. She rode the edge of an enormous wave, threatening to engulf her for only a moment before she gave in to the bliss and fell over the crest into the perfection Danny brought her. Her entire body tensed with thrilling pleasure, her mind went numb and her heart beat so fast she could almost feel it banging against her ribs.

As their tangled bodies slid down the surface of the refrigerator, his laughter rumbled once again in his chest. "I will *never*, ever, look at this kitchen the same way again."

Sadness washed over her and wiped away her afterglow in an instant. She knew he'd go on with his life, and should of course. He'd probably have a slew of women cooking breakfast for him in this kitchen. Tears gathered in her eyes at the thought of another woman touching her Danny the way she had.

He was hers and she was his. Why couldn't he see that?

"I'll never look at *any* kitchen the same again." She gathered her dignity and attempted a level tone, but the lump in her throat caused her voice to crack anyway.

He didn't seem to notice as he laughed again

and hugged her close. When he gradually disconnected their bodies and helped her stand, she felt wobbly and off-kilter and it wasn't all from the sex. She was in love with a man she had no future with.

That sucks.

He held the tips of her fingers in one hand and rubbed the other over his head and around the back of his neck. "Did I ruin your breakfast?"

"I don't know."

She turned her attention to cold over crisp bacon and soupy looking eggs and thought probably, but it had sure been worth it.

Danny left her to return to the living room, but he came back to hand her a pair of thick wool socks and shrugged when she raised a brow at him. "Your feet are always cold."

"Thank you." She didn't know why such a silly gesture meant so much, but it did.

"How about I squeeze us some orange juice, and if breakfast isn't salvageable, I've got frozen waffles and strawberries. I think there's still some whipped cream left from Christmas."

She pulled on the socks and went for the freezer while Danny set up the juicer.

Maybe it was that she'd spent the last three years of her life in constant caregiver mode, not that she would have done it differently, but constantly giving with never having anyone look out for her in return drained her soul in a way she hadn't been sure was fixable.

She'd been told over and over by her mom's nurses that she had to do something for herself to nourish her soul, but she couldn't stop worrying long enough. Now she was at the point that a pair of socks meant everything in the world to her. She curled and flexed her toes inside their new basket of warmth and the emotions overwhelmed her. Tears started to stream down her face, and without warning a loud sob tore from her throat.

Danny was beside her in a heartbeat, wrapping her in his arms and holding her so close she almost couldn't breathe, but she loved it.

Please don't leave me. Please don't let me be alone anymore. I'm dying alone.

She kept the words and the feelings locked inside; she'd die if he found out how needy she was. Don's voice still haunted her dreams, and he'd meant less than nothing to her in comparison.

The hand in her hair pressed her head against his shoulder. She listened to his soothing sounds and words first in her ear, then in her heart. Eventually her sobs turned to sniffles, and he grabbed a cloth, dried her tears and kissed her forehead.

"What happened, sweetheart?"

She shrugged. It was ridiculous that a pair of socks had brought her to tears.

He ran his thumbs over her cheeks, then framed her face in his hands. "You can tell me anything, Caity."

She ran her hand under her nose, sniffed again and pulled away from his tender hold. If she was going to do this, she wasn't about to look at him while she did. "No one's taken care of me in a really long time."

His hands settled on her shoulders. He pulled her tight against his chest in a move that somehow felt even more intimate than when she'd been facing him.

"I've always been the kid who had to make sure everyone else was having a good time before I could enjoy myself, but when mom got sick..." she sighed and felt selfish for even thinking what she was about to say. "It was a whole new level of care giving. It wore me out, Danny, and I had no one to turn to."

Would he think she was a horrible person now? No one would ever understand how hard those years had been on her. They had changed her; in both small and large ways, she was different because of experiencing terminal illness in a loved one. It would take time to assimilate all the ways she was different, and she wasn't sure if anyone would ever want her in as many pieces as she was in.

When Danny didn't instantly reject her—instead kissed her temple and wrapped his arms tighter around her waist, pulling her even firmer against his body, she wondered how on earth this had happened. How had she ever found Danny exactly when she needed him the most?

"What about your friends?"

She shrugged. "They couldn't understand what it was like. No one could unless they'd been there."

"I understand, sweetheart. In a way." He exhaled against her neck and pressed his lips there a moment later. "My ex-wife had emotional issues. We were married four years and I sometimes feel like I spent everyday of those four years taking care of her and never once getting anything in return. By the time she left me, I'm ashamed to say it, but I was more than a little relived."

She turned in a tight circle in his arms, touched his cheeks and softly kissed his mouth. He could never know how much those words meant to her.

"Danny, I love you. I wasn't going to say anything because I know you probably think me irrational or like some silly kid with a crush, but it's so much more, and I'll take care of you every day of the rest of your life if you'll let me."

His grey eyes turned misty, and a tear spilled over the edge and ran down his cheek, landing on her fingertip. She touched the wetness deliberately to see if it were real.

"Caity, my love." He breathed her name and kissed her with soft tenderness until she felt herself melt. "I love you more than I ever imagined possible. If you're a silly kid, then I'm a silly old man. Marry me, Caity. Make a life with me. Have my babies and let's take care of each other. Too soon, I know, but it was all I could do not to say the words a hundred times last night. Marry me. I don't deserve you, but marry me anyway."

She watched him through eyes filling with tears. She didn't know what she'd expected when she'd confessed her love, but for him to feel the same way was more than she could have hoped for. She threw her arms around his neck and held him as tight as she could. His hands moved around her waist, and he lifted her from the floor once more.

"Please tell me that was a yes?"

She pulled her head back, caught a tear that ran down her own cheek and nodded her head.

"Yes. Yes. Yes. Yes!"

He carried her to the living room, laid her gently on the rug before the fire and came down on top of her.

"The world will think we're crazy." He kissed the tip of her nose.

"The world can go to hell." She smiled and laughed as he nuzzled her neck and slipped his thigh between hers.

"I love you, Caity." His dark grey eyes looked into hers with promise. "Last night I made you a woman. Now I intend to make you *my* woman."

"I never want to be anything else."

As he kissed her into oblivion she thought about how her mom had definitely been right, because she loved Danny Carter with all her heart and soul and she just knew it. One more thought slipped its way into her conscious as Danny slipped inside her.

This has been one hell of a New Year's resolution.

Printed in the United States
144050LV00001B/32/P

9 781601 541963